CAPTIVE
IN ISLAM

Murshed Parveen
(Urmi)
God Bless you

CAPTIVE IN ISLAM

ARLINE WESTMEIER

ReadersMagnet, LLC

All proceeds from this book will go to
NLCC (aka Center to The Unreached).
https://www.ctunreached.com/

Table of Contents

Introduction

In 2003 when New Life Christian Center (NLCC), now known as the Center to the Unreached (CTU), began their emphasis on reaching the Unreached People Groups in Queens, NY, most of whom were Muslim, no one was sure how to go about doing it. David Westmeier, the pastor of NLCC, was born to missionaries Karl and Arline Westmeier, serving with the Christian and Missionary Alliance (C&MA) in Colombia and later in Puerto Rico, but there were very few Muslims in these countries.

When services ended in the mosque, located one half-block from their Queens church, the Muslims filled the street in front of the church or sat on the steps leading up to the church door. When the church service ended, the Christians walked around them without even trying to talk to them. Christians and Muslims simply did not interact.

While he was studying at Nyack College, David had worked in a motel where his boss was Muslim. He gave his boss a Bible, and his boss gave him a Qur'an. He tried to share his faith with his boss, but it did not go very well. His boss did not seem to understand what he was trying to share.

During that time, David learned that according to the Qur'an, when anyone dies, he or she automatically goes to hell and Allah will decide how long they need to stay and suffer to balance out the wrongs they committed in their lifetime. No one could be sure how long that would be until after they had died.

David was very concerned about the Muslim people standing outside their church. He wanted to gather a group of Christians to come with him to talk to the Muslims, but no one would go with him. They would talk to Latin people who looked like themselves and who spoke their Spanish language, but not to the Muslims.

Eventually, he decided to go by himself. He got some tracts about the way of salvation and crossed the street to give them to a group of Muslim men. But the encounter ended with the Muslim men telling him that the Bible is corrupted, and that God could not have had a son.

David's sister Ruthie was teaching English as a Second Language in Tibet for 2 years. When she returned, she joined NLCC and took part in their weekly street evangelism, their prayer walks, and their times of fasting (several times, a few of them fasted for 40 days). They were doing a spiritual battle with the darkness around them that held the people captive so that they could not understand that Jesus had opened the direct way to God.

One day as David and Ruthie were out on street evangelism, they could not find the place for which they were looking. "So," Ruthie said, "David did his 'usual thing' when out on street evangelism. He simply walked up to the apartment building beside us and looked for any apartment with a name that sounded Muslim and rang the doorbell." Neither of them could have imagined how completely "God-arranged" this whole little evening visit was.

A very dressed-up woman came to the door, and Ruthie introduced themselves. "Hi. My name is Ruthie, and this is my brother David. What is your name?"

"My name is Urmi."[1]

"We have a book for you. Have you ever read the *Injil* (Gospel)?"

Very hesitantly, the woman took the book.

"Read it," Ruthie said kindly. "I'll come back next week and see what you think about it."

The woman told Ruthie about the store she and her husband owned. That was where she spent most of her time. Ruthie could visit her there and then they could talk. In the following weeks, David and Ruthie continued to visit Urmi, and a friendship developed. No one could imagine what God had in store for that friendship and the many lives that would be changed.

---

1   All Muslim names have been changed for security purposes.

Chapter 1

The Marriage Proposal

"Let's get them married," the little four-year-old girls giggled as they hugged their dolls. "Mine will be the bride, because yours is a man doll," said little Urmi.

"Yes," agreed her friend, "and we'll make a big wedding party for them, with lots of food to eat," she whispered.

"Let's do it for real! I'll ask my Amma (mother) to cook a real party dinner, and we'll invite all our friends." The little girls' wedding plan for their dolls was exciting. Soon they had talked Urmi's Amma into cooking real food for the dolls' wedding feast and to invite many friends.

Urmi's Abba (Father) was working far away from home as an accountant with the Bangladeshi Army. He began working with the army in 1967 before Bangladesh had its independence. When India became independent from Britain, Pakistan also became its own country, but it was made up of West and East Pakistan (now Bangladesh). In 1968, Abba moved to West Pakistan, and Amma followed a few years later. In 1971, Bangladesh won its independence, but Amma and Abba stayed in Pakistan until 1973. While they were in Pakistan the family grew. Amma and Abba returned with three children.

When they returned to Bangladesh, Abba continued to work in the Army. He would get reassigned every 4 years. At first Amma would pack up all the children and move with Abba, but after having 5 children she did not feel these changes were good for them. They decided to buy a house in the city where the children could get a good education and settle down. Abba would continue to go where he was assigned and then come home to visit every 4 to 6 months.

Most of the time, Amma was at home alone with the children and felt lonesome. The little girls' wedding plans for their dolls gave her some unexpected excitement.

From little Urmi's point of view, her Amma was always looking and thinking about finding a better man, one who was romantic, loved parties, and liked having a good time. Her father on the other hand, was pensive, conscientious, and detail-oriented.

Urmi missed her Abba and wished he could be there for the dolls' party. She slipped, quiet as a mouse, into her place in the corner under the top bunk of their bed. There she could sit and think and study. No one disturbed her there.

For little Urmi, it seemed Amma was always angry and discontented, constantly looking for someone who would make a better husband than her father: someone educated, romantic, and who would have a high paying and more respectable job.

Urmi was 8 years old and going to school when one of Abba's good friends came to visit them from far out in the country, where there was little food and no good schools. His son, Omar, had begged and insisted for so long to come to their town to go to school that his Abba finally consented to ask Urmi's Amma if he could stay with her family to study.

Omar said over and over that he would kill himself if he couldn't stay. To show that he really meant it and would actually kill himself, several times he ran to the village pond to throw himself into the water. The villagers ran after him shouting that he shouldn't do it. They pulled him back from the water and brought him back to where his Abba was still negotiating with Urmi's Amma.

Although Omar was only 11 years old, he studied hard and soon was at the top of his class. He decided he would find a way to never, ever break off his studies again. He talked to Urmi's mother about his plans to finish his studies and make a lot of money. He would kill himself before he would give up his studies. He had to find some way to keep from being sent back into the country.

Soon Omar and Amma began making plans. Amma saw in Omar a brilliant, promising youth who would become a wealthy, prominent man: the perfect husband for her daughter. So, their plans grew, and they were not playing with dolls!

"Why are you doing this, Amma," thought Urmi when she heard them talk. "I'm only 8 years old, and I want to go to school and learn things. Omar is a boy and I don't like him, and he's only 11 years old. I don't want to get married to him."

Urmi could think these things, but in her Muslim culture in Bangladesh, she could never say them to her Amma. Being a child, she could never protest her Amma's plans. A child was not allowed to have any different opinion or even to look at her Amma when she spoke. Any child who did not stand with downcast eyes or who dared to protest when spoken to by a parent was severely punished.

"Why is she doing this to me?" thought the confused little girl as she crept back to her corner. "I don't understand. She knows I don't want to get married. Why does she do this to me?"

The plans being made for her were just like those they had made for the wedding of her dolls. Her Amma was even planning a big feast just like the one she had made for the dolls. "What happened to me? When did I become a doll?"

"I have talked to Omar's family," Amma said, finishing the topic. "They will be coming to visit us next week and arrange for the wedding. You must be very kind and pleasant with them. Omar will be an educated, romantic husband for you with an excellent job. It is all arranged."

Omar's family came the next week to talk with Amma. They talked with the local Imam, who came to the house immediately and performed the marriage. Now Urmi was married and couldn't do anything about it. She went back to her corner and wished her Abba would come.

"I will write Abba a letter and tell him what is happening," thought Urmi. Amma was illiterate. But Abba had taught Urmi to write what her Amma dictated, how to address the letter, go to the post-office and buy a stamp, and send it off. Urmi wrote all the family letters to her father. Now she wrote him a very special letter that Amma did not know about and told him everything that had happened. She slipped it into the mail unnoticed.

After she was married, her world changed. The children would point at her and laugh and snigger,

"Look. She's married." "How is it?" others would laugh. Now when she walked to school no one wanted to walk with her.

When Abba received Urmi's letter, he immediately arranged to come home. He was furious about the marriage and shouted at Amma, "This cannot be. I will talk to them and put them all in jail. I won't let this happen to my daughter!"

Suddenly Amma's voice became very quiet. Urmi had never heard Amma speak quietly. She always screamed, but now she talked so quietly that Urmi could not understand what she was saying.

"It makes no difference," shouted Abba. "It cannot be. I will divorce them."

Abba went to the local registrar to perform an official divorce, and Urmi was no longer married. She felt so grateful to her Abba. Now she could continue going to school.

Chapter 2

Learning to be Muslim

Eight-year-old Urmi giggled. She knew where her Abba's glasses were hiding. Everyone was looking for them: her Abba, her Amma, her sister and her three little brothers, although they couldn't help much. After all, they were the little ones. Urmi was the oldest of the children; she could see the top of her Abba's head. There she found his glasses! How they all laughed. Abba and everyone had been searching for his glasses, but they had not seen the top of his head.

For Urmi, this was the normal evening ritual. Abba usually had trouble with his glasses. He said he could see better without them, except to read. He read funny words when he read stories without his glasses.

Amma was always there for the five children. She cooked their meals, washed their clothes, and in the afternoons bathed all five of them. After that they would eat, and then came the time for their schoolwork.

Amma would often scream and yell at them. When Amma began yelling, Abba would simply leave the house. Urmi was the oldest of the five children, so she protected her little brothers when Amma wanted to hit them with a stick or a ruler. They had many broken rulers in their house.

Amma taught the girls many practical things. They learned how to cook delicious meals, and how to deal with the many beggars who came to the door asking for food. One time when a beggar came looking for food, Amma was busy and asked Urmi to give the beggar some rice.

Urmi found the rice pot had a large amount of rice. Abba had always taught that giving to the poor was a good deed, so she simply dumped a potful of rice into the astonished beggar's bag. When Amma found out how much rice Urmi had given the beggar, she used this to teach Urmi how to treat beggars.

"You must never give a beggar a large amount of anything, because then they will become dependent on you. With this rice, you should only have given one or two handfuls. When you give them so much, they will begin to think that you will always give them all the rice they need for their family. Then when you don't have that much to give, they will think you are cheating them and they will get very angry, even destructive.

"With this rice you could have given a little bit to everyone who came. In the next houses they will get a little bit more. By the time they come to the end of the village they will have gathered enough to feed their whole family."

This was a lesson Urmi never forgot. Even now, she gives only a little bit of something to every beggar who comes.

When Abba took a nap, Urmi would gently massage his temples to keep him asleep. When their schoolwork was finished, Abba would close the books, push up his glasses, and begin to tell them about Islam or read from the Qur'an.

Her father was pensive, conscientious, and detailed. He was always on time and very thorough with his many rituals. He carefully followed the "Five Pillars" of Islam: 1) A declaration of faith in Allah (shahada); 2) five daily prayers (salat); 3) fasting (saum); 4) almsgiving (zakat); and 5) a pilgrimage to Mecca (hajj).

Abba was carefully doing the five pillars, but he had not yet gone on hajj. Allah had commanded every Muslim to go to Mecca in Saudi Arabia once in their lifetime unless they were too sick to go or so poor that they could not save enough money for the expensive trip.

Abba's prayers were always done in the faithful Muslim way. Five times at the designated times, he rolled out his prayer mat facing Mecca, and getting down on his knees with his face pressed against the mat, he prayed the designated prayers to Allah. Every day after the morning prayer he would recite some Surahs (chapters) from the Qur'an in Arabic.

Although Abba, like most Muslims outside of Arabic speaking countries did not speak Arabic, so he knew it was important to recite the Surahs every day to receive Allah's blessing. To Urmi it always sounded as though he were singing a song. She would wake up every morning to the sound of her father's voice. She would lay in bed thinking he sounded just like a bird singing its song in the morning. She knew she was protected and safe because her Abba was doing what Allah required.

Thinking of Abba always made Urmi smile. He had often told her the story of her birth. Abba's mother had died when he was 6 years old; he always longed for a mother. He asked Allah over and over for a little girl. Abba always talked to Allah, and, like every good Muslim, he saw himself as Allah's slave. He did everything Allah wanted. Now he told his wife and friends that he knew Allah would reward him with a daughter.

"How can you be so sure it will be a girl?" his friends asked.

"I know because I am doing everything Allah wants me to do and he will reward me with a daughter." He was so sure, Abba told her, that when her Amma was in the hospital giving birth, he went out and bought many beautiful clothes to celebrate the arrival of their little girl. Although she had a younger sister and three younger brothers, Urmi always felt special to her father.

Chapter 3

The Balancing Scale

Allah has a balancing scale, Abba taught them. Everything bad that they did was put on one side and everything good on the other side. If the bad side weighed more than the good side when they died, they would go to hell and suffer until they had outweighed the bad.

But no one could know for sure what Allah would decide about their scale until after their death. Even Muhammad did not know when he died and went to hell how long he would need to suffer or how soon he could go on to paradise.

Abba always taught the children what was *Haram* (sinful) in the Muslim religion because he didn't want the bad side of their scale to weigh too much. He explained that lying, stealing, and not obeying your parents were very bad. Urmi was not allowed to speak to boys before she got married. It was also important to dress appropriately. Urmi always wore a scarf over her clothes from the time she turned 12. The neighbors would comment on the girls who didn't wear their scarves. Urmi forgot one time, and after having the neighbors shame her she ran home and got her scarf. She made sure this would never happen again.

They were taught other things as well. Urmi learned that most of TV was *Haram*. The news and some children's educational programs were ok, but all movies (including the theater), dramas, or TV shows were forbidden under this rule. This was difficult for Urmi because she liked a lot of TV shows.

At night, an American program called Dallas was shown. It came on at 11 p.m. She would wait for her mother to fall asleep and then she would sneak out and watch it. Sometimes Amma woke up and caught her. She would start yelling and screaming, reminding Urmi about school, because to Amma it wasn't that important that it was *Haram*. Urmi made sure Abba never found out, because she knew he would be very disappointed with her disobedience. He would also worry about her balance scale.

The good that would weigh the most on the balance scale would be to go on Hajj. Abba was eager to go on Hajj as soon as he could get everything ready, but his children needed to be older before he could be free to go.

Abba told the children that if they would not steal or lie, and if they did other good works, such as fasting during Ramadan, giving to the poor, or going on Hajj, they would only go to hell on their way to paradise. But if they did not practice their religion, they would go to hell to stay.

Little Urmi just knew that Abba was so good and so thorough with the requirements of his religion that he would surely go straight to heaven and take her with him. Even though she did not pray five times a day, she knew that her Abba loved her too much to go to paradise without her. This always gave her peace (and an excuse to stay in bed instead of getting up for morning prayers).

Abba had run away from his home when he was 11 years old and later left their village. At age 18, he joined the army because it provided a good salary, with good benefits. He got housing, free healthcare, and many opportunities for advancement. While in the army, Abba worked as an undercover agent, but he never took bribes. When people asked why he wouldn't accept any money, he always answered, "It would hurt my religion"

Amma's family was not nearly so devout. They were not as precise in doing their prayers. They prayed, but only two or three times a day instead of five times.

Nani[2] (maternal grandmother) was a very warm person. She told stories from the Qur'an about Noah, who had a big boat, and *Isa* (Jesus), who did many miracles, but had no Abba. For little Urmi, this was unthinkable. She couldn't imagine not having her Abba. Why? How was this possible? According to her understanding everyone had an Abba and Amma.

---

2   Dadi is the paternal grandmother (who died when Urmi's Abba was six years old), and Dada is the paternal grandfather. Nana was the maternal grandfather and Nani, the maternal grandmother (who told the stories about Isa).

"Well," explained Nani (Grandma). "Allah wanted Mary to have *Isa*. All Allah had to do was say 'Be' for anything he wanted, and it would be so." For little Urmi, *Isa* (Jesus) was a very special prophet. He did many miracles. When Nani told stories about *Isa*, it was a very special time. But the stories about *Isa* in the Qur'an were all very, very short.

Urmi would often ask Nani to pray for her. "It is good to ask me to pray for you because unless you ask me to pray, I cannot pray for you. No one can pray for anyone who has not asked for prayer. You must always ask. If I pray for you when you don't ask, then it will cause me spiritual problems."

Urmi never understood what kind of problems this would cause. Nani would pray with candles and sometimes fruit in the middle of the night. Urmi never saw any other Muslims pray like this. She often wondered if her Abba and her Nani actually practiced the same religion. Nani would do all the regular Muslim rituals, but then she would pray these extra strange prayers.

Sometimes, Urmi would ask Nani why she did these extra prayers with candles, fruits, and flowers but Nani answered as all the adults always answered. "Do not ask about religion, and do not ask about what I'm doing." She did this all in secret in the room Urmi would share with her when she visited. Urmi was always curious about what she was doing but Nani never explained.

Nani did explain that Urmi was not allowed to tell Abba or Amma, because Nani would get in trouble. Urmi was very careful not to tell anyone about Nani's prayers. Urmi would often ask Nani to pray for her when she had a problem like a headache or a test the next day. Nani would start whispering a prayer that Urmi couldn't understand because she prayed it so quietly. "What are you praying? Teach me, I want to learn to pray for others," Urmi would ask. Nani would say, "Don't tell anyone but I'm praying in the name of Murshid." Nani was always afraid she would get in trouble if anyone found out.

The Qur'an was considered such a holy book, that it was kept on the highest shelf in the house. That shelf was considered to be so important that nothing else could be put there. The Qur'an had to be covered with a special cloth so no dust would touch it. Before anyone could touch it or read from it, they had to first wash their hands and then their mouths and noses three times. Then their feet also had to be washed three times. Urmi learned that there was a special way to wash her hands, face, and feet to be clean before reading the Qur'an and doing her prayers. There were surahs that had to be recited every step of the washing process. It took a long time and lots of practice before Urmi and her brothers and sister could do it right.

After that they must change into especially clean clothes over which *suras* had been recited while they were being washed. This made the clothes especially clean to read the Qur'an. Afterwards, these special clothes were folded and kept in a clean place for the next reading. It was important that the Qur'an would not touch an ordinary object like a table. There was a special wooden stand that was placed on the table in order to hold the Qur'an. Urmi quickly learned that the Qur'an was the most special object in the house, and it had to be treated with great reverence.

It was so important to Abba that the children learned to recite the Qur'an correctly that he paid a female Imam, Noorjahan, to come to the family to teach the children how to form the Arabic letters. She was rather rough and often screamed at them when they didn't make them exactly right. Although she was an Imam, she never led the prayers in a mosque. Only a man could do that. Until recently, only the men went to the mosque. Now the women may also go, but they need to sit apart in a special place just for women so the men would not be distracted from their prayers.

Abba taught them the correct pronunciation but never the meaning of the Arabic words. The children quickly learned not to ask about the meaning. "When you pray in Arabic," he said, "Allah will always hear you, because that is his language; even when you don't understand what you are saying, Allah will understand. If you know how to recite the Surahs in Arabic you will receive blessings from Allah," replied Abba.

Abba explained that the pronunciation of the Arabic words needed to be exactly right, because it was the holy language of Allah. Getting the pronunciation perfectly right was very important. During the month of Ramadan, everyone fasted from sunrise to sundown. Abba and Amma woke everyone up at 3:00 a.m. to eat an enormous meal before sunrise. After that they could not eat or drink, not even swallow their own saliva, until sundown. At sundown, the family broke their fast at a special meal called Fitar. Amma would prepare lots of special foods that were only eaten during Ramadan.

Urmi loved Ramadan because she loved the food Amma would prepare. Urmi had learned that there were special dishes that could only be eaten if you had fasted at home. She was very careful to fast because she loved to try all the food. Urmi's favorite dish was beguni, which was eggplant that was mixed in chickpea flour with spices and then fried. Urmi knew if she didn't fast she wouldn't be allowed to eat. She would make sure to fast, but sometimes her brothers would not fast. She always tried to encourage them to fast, too.

During Ramadan the days would be spent praying and reading the Qur'an and visiting friends and relatives. Urmi really liked to pray because then she wouldn't feel her hunger so much. The more she prayed, the less hungry she felt.

On the twenty-ninth day of Ramadan the whole town would go outside and look for the moon. Abba explained that if you could see the moon then Ramadan was over. Sometimes Urmi would see the moon on the twenty-ninth day but sometimes she wouldn't see it until the thirtieth day. She always hoped it would be seen on the twenty-ninth day because that would be the last day of Ramadan and *Eid al-Fitr* would begin.

Eid al-Fitr was a huge, fun holiday. The whole town would celebrate. Everyone would cook the most special foods. Everyone was dressed in their best clothes. Abba and Amma would get the children ready. Everyone would get up early to take a shower and put on their new clothes, make-up, and perfume. Abba would go to the mosque with Urmi's brothers. Amma and the girls would stay at home preparing the food for the celebration. All the doors of all the houses were continually open and families would go from house to house.

Urmi would get her brothers and sister together and go from house to house. In every house they were given food. In the morning, it would be sweet foods, but in the evening, it was spicy foods. She knew that she needed to make sure that her brothers and sister only ate a little bit because at the next house they would need to eat more. This was her favorite holiday. Everyone was so friendly, everyone hugged, and they were all happy and smiling. They would greet each other saying "Eid Mubarak," which means "Happy Eid."

A few days before the end of Ramadan, the family would buy new clothes; the children could help pick out what they wanted. Urmi always picked the most beautiful dress, but that was also the most expensive one. Amma wanted to save money and refused to pay that much for a dress. Urmi sobbed and sobbed and wouldn't eat.

On one such occasion Abba came into Urmi's room where she was lying on her bed sobbing. He asked her what was wrong. She said that she wanted the pretty dress for *Eid* and Amma would not buy it for her because it was too expensive. Abba went out and told Amma to buy the dress. The next day Amma bought the dress, and Urmi was happy.

Like most children, Urmi did not like to help around the house. When Amma insisted that she come to help, she would often go to her bed and cry. Once Abba came in and quietly laid his hand on her head and eventually said, "It's OK. It really is OK. She is your Amma and has the right to ask that you help her with the work."

When she had quieted down, he said gently, "Go now and help your Amma." And since it was her Abba who said that, she got up to do what her Amma was asking.

Urmi was not always honest with her Abba. Amma had asked her to help with cleaning the house. But Urmi sat at the table pretending to be doing homework. Amma knew she didn't have homework and simply didn't want to help. They were arguing when Abba came in and asked her why she was pouting.

"I'm sitting here trying to do my homework, and Amma keeps interrupting me and I can't concentrate." Abba told Amma to let her finish her homework and not disturb her. Urmi knew she had lied and remembers it to this day.

Chapter 4

Becoming a Wife and Mother

Now Urmi was almost nine years old and divorced. Although this meant she could continue going to school, her mother never let down her quest to find an educated, romantic husband for her daughter. Although many people visited their home, none seemed to suit her Amma.

Amma hired a teacher for the children. Apparently, he was a good teacher, but Urmi felt he was constantly staring at her. It seemed she could not get away from him. She finally told her mother about this and she dismissed him. The same thing was happening with the men on the streets and in school, which made her very uncomfortable.

When Urmi was 15, Amma's water pump in the house broke, and two young men came to repair it. One of them, named Shahid, kept returning over and over to see if it was really fixed right. Eventually, he almost seemed like one of the family.

Urmi didn't really like him. He would come to visit all the time, and she would be angry because he was always there. She couldn't express her feelings, but she avoided him as much as she could. For two years, Shahid wrote little love poems to Urmi, even though she refused to pay any attention to him. But he persisted, and although she continued to ignore him, she began to like his poems. Later he would tell her that the more she rejected him, the more he felt attracted to her.

Shahid's family, with eight children, lived far out in the country where there were few jobs and very little money. They had no good schools and very little to eat. Like Urmi's Dada (Grandfather), Shahid's Abba did not want to waste too much money on his children because they would just grow up and leave.

They concentrated on sending one of the boys to study for a career with the thought that he would then help them with the others. But when he graduated and found a good job, he got married and forgot about the rest.

Urmi continued sitting in her corner studying, not talking to anyone. When two years had passed, Shahid brought his parents to meet Urmi. His mother did not approve of Urmi because she was too young. But mainly she complained because Urmi's skin was too dark. She was a lighter-skinned lady and didn't want her son to marry someone darker than herself.

Amma was quite pleased. Shahid was a handsome man and would surely make her daughter a good husband. Amma and Shahid began to make plans. Amma and Abba went to visit Shahid's family. Abba thought he was ok but wanted her to finish her education first; he didn't want this marriage to happen too soon. Urmi was never really told what was going on. She was asked to go to visit his family, but she wasn't really interested. She didn't realize that they were discussing marriage.

At this time Shahid was not employed full time. Occasionally he would help his brother in his plumbing business. His parents didn't want him to marry until he had a full-time income. He also didn't feel he was ready to marry, but Amma had decided to move to the capital city, Dhaka, because Abba had been transferred there. In Dhaka, the education, lifestyle, and opportunities were much better.

Shahid was afraid he was going to lose Urmi if she moved. He wanted to have an official commitment before they moved even though he wasn't prepared financially to have a family. He explained to Amma that he wanted to get married, but they would not start a family for another year. Urmi could go with Amma to Dhaka and finish her education. Amma liked this plan because she thought Shahid would make the perfect husband, and she didn't want to lose this opportunity.

Shahid's family refused to participate in this plan. They didn't feel he was ready to have a family, and they would not support this marriage. They knew that in the end, the financial responsibility would fall on them if he had children without a job. Shahid convinced Amma to go along with the plan even though his family disagreed.

Shahid realized that no one had spoken to Urmi about the situation. He asked Amma if he could talk to her. Shahid sat down to talk with Urmi. This was the first conversation they would have. Shahid spoke to Urmi and explained the plan. They would get married, and she would go to Dhaka with her family and finish her education there. He explained they would not have a big celebration yet but just register the marriage before she moved to Dhaka. When he was ready to have a family with her, then they would have a big celebration. "Do you agree? What do you think?"

Urmi was very scared and didn't know what to think. She wasn't happy about the arrangement, but she knew she couldn't disagree with Amma's plan. Urmi really wanted to go to Dhaka and finish her secondary education (11th and 12th grades) before she got married. Urmi answered as she had been taught all her life: "My Amma has made a decision. She knows what is best for me. I have no choice."

Shahid insisted that she tell him her own decision, but Urmi refused. The truth was that she liked his poems and was starting to like him, but she didn't want to give up her education. She was afraid to tell him the truth.

Amma didn't want to delay the wedding. So the Imam came to the house and performed the marriage registration in front of about 15 guests. No one from Shahid's family came. Very quickly the ceremony was over and at the age of 17, Urmi found herself married to a 24-year-old-man she hardly knew. Two days later, Amma, Urmi, and the children flew to Dhaka to live with Abba.

The army had provided an apartment in a five-story building for the family. Urmi loved the apartment because it was bigger and more luxurious than the house in the village. Unbelievably, all the children had their own rooms, and there was a large balcony and a roof to relax on. It was open and sunny.

Often people would stop by to visit. They would knock and Amma would invite the guests in. If it was someone from their family, they would stay for a week or two, and a neighbor would get a big snack. Abba's co-workers would come to visit him, and Amma would make sure there were always snacks available.

It was important that all guests got something to eat when they visited. No one would call ahead; every visit was a surprise. Urmi loved the freedom and openness of this lifestyle. She loved being in the city. She thought it was much better than the village.

Urmi began 11th grade in Dhaka. She loved her school. She didn't tell anyone she was married. She was too embarrassed because no one in her classes was married. She began making new friends. They would get together and study or go out for picnics. She was involved in sports and the drama club. She had really found her place. It was such a happy time.

Shahid began to take the 8-hour bus ride to visit Urmi in Dhaka once a month. These visits were always a surprise because at that time no one had a telephone. They could only communicate by letter. Shahid loved to write his new wife letters. Sometimes he would write her a letter on the bus ride home. He wrote poems and love letters. Urmi felt so special every time she got one. Every day she would watch for the mailman, because she knew he was going to bring her a letter from Shahid. Sometimes, Urmi would write him back. She missed him and always looked forward to his visits.

After six months she got pregnant, but since no one had explained anything about pregnancy to her, she didn't realize it for about four months. Neither Shahid nor her Amma accepted the pregnancy. They tried in every way to force her to abort the baby. Amma and Shahid said, "Amma has spent a lot of money for you to finish your secondary education and you can have a baby anytime. You will be wasting her money. You need to get an abortion and finish your education." Both Shahid and Amma were angry, yelling and cursing at her.

"I will never abort my baby," Urmi insisted. "You cannot make me do it. I will finish my education after one year. Killing my baby is a big deal. I won't do it." For the first time Urmi found her voice and refused to do what Amma was trying to force her to do.

When Amma realized that Urmi was not going to change her mind, she screamed at Shahid. "You need to be responsible for her. Take your wife and baby home and take care of them. We agreed to help her get her education, but we did not agree to support your baby. You need to be responsible and act like a husband and a father. Take her and start a family. If you didn't want a baby yet, why were you coming once a month? Take your wife and go! You're the father."

Shahid answered, "I need her to abort the baby and finish her education. I do not have a job, and I can't take this responsibility." They argued back and forth, but Urmi continued to refuse to get an abortion. Shahid became angrier and angrier.

Shahid screamed at Urmi, "You are not listening to us. You are making this decision on your own, so I'm leaving. I will have nothing to do with this." He was very angry and immediately went to the bus station and left her. An hour later, he returned to see if she had changed her mind, but she had not. Shahid walked out, and Urmi did not know if she would hear from him again.

Urmi still hoped she would get a letter from him explaining what was going on. She waited every day for the mailman, but no letter came. She held to this hope for three months, and then she realized she was never going to get a letter.

Urmi cried and cried. She felt all alone with her baby. In a few months she went from having friends in school, a social life, and what she described as the best time of her life, to being abandoned by her husband, pregnant, and rejected by her mother.

Her mother was so angry because Urmi would not obey her that she refused to speak to her. She felt as though her mother treated her like a slave. She was afraid to ask her mother for more food when she was hungry because of the pregnancy. Amma ignored her all the time and Urmi wondered how a mother could treat her own daughter like a stepchild. Urmi felt as though she had committed a crime by choosing to keep her baby.

One time, Nani came to visit the house. When she heard Urmi's story, she cried with her and tried to comfort her. She told her it was going to be ok. She was very angry with Amma and Shahid. Instead of going home after two weeks like she usually did, Nani stayed for two months so Urmi would not be so alone.

She always made sure Urmi had the extra food she needed. Nani would tell her Abba to bring fruit from the store for Urmi, but she would make sure that Amma never found out because Amma got angry every time anyone was nice to Urmi. This was the only time during her pregnancy that Urmi felt cared for.

After dinner, Urmi would often go to the roof on the sixth floor of the house and think about her life.

"Why did my husband love me so much before getting married, and now he has abandoned me? Why? What did I do wrong?"

At 18, Urmi had tried to do everything right. She obeyed her mother when she got married, she didn't have boyfriends like other girls did, she was obedient, and she studied hard. Her only dream was to finish her education, and now she had lost even that. Everyone abandoned her. Even her own mother. Why was she suffering so much? Why did she have to live this life? She couldn't make sense of it. She saw that other families were excited about having a baby. She didn't understand why nobody wanted her to have her baby.

On the roof, she would think about what a terrible person she must be to be treated like this. It must all be her fault. Maybe she wasn't beautiful enough, or good enough, or smart enough. Many times she contemplated committing suicide. One day it was just too much and she decided to jump off the roof. She couldn't handle this life anymore. She went to the edge of the roof and looked down from the 6th floor.

She knew that if she jumped her suffering would end. Everyone would be happy. Her mother's suffering would be relieved, and her husband would be free and wouldn't have to worry about her or the baby anymore. She was happy this would soon be over.

Suddenly, she heard a small voice saying, "No, no. Don't jump. You have been fighting with your mother and husband to keep the baby. If you jump you will kill the baby. That doesn't make any sense." Urmi instantly knew that this was not a good solution. She couldn't kill the baby.

Years later, after she knew Jesus, looking back at that time, she realized Jesus was there with her, giving her the strength to stand up to Amma and Shahid and refuse to get an abortion and then stopping her from committing suicide. She realized that it was Jesus who was speaking to her on the roof, even though she didn't yet know Him.

When Urmi was eight months pregnant, Amma realized that her anger was not going to change Urmi's mind. The baby would be born no matter what. She stopped being angry at Urmi and decided to accept the baby. As the time of birth neared, Urmi became more and more afraid about what was going to happen to her baby. Her husband was gone, Urmi didn't have a job, and no one was there to provide for the baby.

Money was always tight in the house because her father's salary had to cover the expenses of five children. She couldn't imagine how her baby would be provided for. Amma would comfort her saying, "Don't worry. After the baby is born, I'll take care of the baby while you finish your education."

Urmi was adamant about one thing. "Amma, the first thing I have to do after the baby is born is get a divorce. I don't want to be married to that man anymore. He abandoned me and his baby. What kind of man does this? I don't want to continue my life with him. He's dead to me."

Amma was very angry at Shahid as well. Every day she would talk about him, "As soon the baby is born, I will take you to get a divorce. I don't understand that man, for two years he came to my house begging to marry you, madly in love, and then he leaves you when you get pregnant. I made a mistake allowing him to marry you. My punishment will be to care for your baby while you continue your education. You can see yourself as single and enjoy your life." Every day

Amma would tell this to Urmi. Urmi started to feel some hope.

When Urmi went into labor, Amma took her to the hospital. The doctor was shocked that Amma had Urmi marry at 17, and now at 18 she was already having a baby. She told Amma, "You are a terrible mother. People don't do things like that anymore."

Urmi had a little girl and named her Emily. She was beautiful. But unlike Urmi when she was born, little Emily had no doting Abba who cheered her arrival.

Amma did as she promised and took over the care of the baby. Urmi looked forward to getting her divorce and starting school again. The 11th grade would start in two months, and Urmi began preparing to go back. She felt like she had her life back. Many people came to see the baby, bringing gifts and congratulating Urmi.

They would often ask about the baby's daddy. Amma was embarrassed about what Shahid had done and would lie saying, "He is out of the country working." She told Urmi, "If anyone asks you about your husband, tell them that he is out of the country working." The situation was very embarrassing for the family. Things like this did not happen in Bangladesh.

When Emily was forty days old, Amma went to answer one of the many knocks on the door. Urmi was in the other room playing with the baby. When she heard Amma start to yell, Urmi was worried about what was happening and ran to her Amma in the other room. As she got nearer she heard her Amma yelling, "Why are you here? We thought you were dead. You are a dead person to us." Urmi saw Shahid standing outside the door with his head down. She was so angry that she turned around, took the baby to her room, and locked the door. She never wanted him to see the baby.

She could hear that Amma and Shahid were talking in the living room. Urmi wondered why Amma would even let him in. She was so angry. After a couple of hours, Amma knocked on the bedroom door, and Urmi refused to open it. She said, "I don't want him to see my baby. He has no right to see her. He doesn't deserve it. I'm the one who suffered while he was living his life, and now he wants to see the baby. After eight months? No way."

Amma said she just wanted to come in and speak to her. Urmi let her come in since Shahid was not at the door with her. Amma sat down on the bed and explained some things to Urmi. "Look, he left on his own and came back on his own; we didn't invite him. He is asking for forgiveness and a second chance. The reality is that Emily needs a father in this society. People will be talking about her all her life if she doesn't have a father around. You know how it is. I think we should give him a chance for Emily's sake. Calm down, meet with him, and see what happens."

Urmi was convinced to give Shahid another chance, but she was clear with Amma that she was going to stay in Dhaka with her and finish her education like they had originally agreed to do. Urmi was clear that Shahid could not stay. Amma agreed to this.

Amma then asked Shahid to come into the room. "Urmi, please forgive me. I'm sorry. Please give me a second chance," he begged.

When Urmi saw him, she felt all the hurt and rejection again. The pain was more than she could bear. He had acted like he loved her so much, and then he abandoned her. She couldn't believe he could do something like this, but he had done it anyway. All these feelings turned to anger at the sight of him.

"Why did you leave me? What did I do to you? Why did you punish me? You didn't even write. I waited for three months hoping to get a letter from you. You always sent letters. Why didn't you write and explain your situation? You left me all alone." She began sobbing loudly. She just wished he would leave.

Shahid didn't defend himself. He took everything she said and then hugged her and tried to calm her down. He admitted he was wrong.

"I was angry and wasn't thinking. I don't have a job, and I wasn't ready for a baby. What I did was wrong, and it wasn't fair to you. Please give me a second chance to be a good husband and father."

Urmi began to calm down and understand. She decided to forgive him and give him the second chance he was asking for. She told him about her concerns about having enough money to raise Emily. She explained that her father's job couldn't support her four siblings and another baby. She asked him what he was planning to do to support the baby.

"Please understand that I still don't have a job, and I can't support you yet, so please stay here with your mother and father. My plan is to go overseas and get a job to support the three of us."

"Seriously, Shahid, you come after eight months with empty hands. You didn't even bring a gift for your daughter. Even strangers who have come to visit and see the baby have brought her gifts. I don't understand you. You're her father."

Shahid immediately put his hand in his pocket and took out all the money he had and gave it to her. It wasn't much, but with that money, they went shopping for the baby. He bought her some clothes and a can of powdered milk. Two days later he left to go back to his parents' house. Urmi didn't get any letters or money from him after he left. Urmi's forgiveness turned to anger when he disappeared again. She completely gave up on him.

"Don't be angry at Shahid," Amma said, "it is because he has no job. You must just forgive him. He comes and goes however he wants to. Your daughter needs a father, so you need to forgive him." But Amma was also very angry at Shahid because of the way he treated her daughter.

After that Urmi wasn't even that upset because she figured it was more of the same and she wasn't expecting much from him anymore. She realized she couldn't count on him and needed to make her way alone. She started to look for a job and enrolled in the higher secondary school. It was difficult to find a job without a high school diploma. Every night Urmi would cry out to Allah and ask Him to help her feed her baby, help her find a job, and help her finish her education. She felt at times like He was the only one who understood her.

After three months Shahid showed up at the door and handed Urmi the money in his pocket. She just shook her head and showed him the can of powdered milk he bought the last time. "Do you really think this is enough to feed your daughter for three months? I wish this milk would give birth to another can of milk. Then maybe one can would be enough for your daughter to survive for three months."

"My father has been buying milk for your daughter," continued Urmi. "Amma had to go to her village and sell a cow so I can go to school and feed our baby. I never ask them for anything for Emily because I am so ashamed that her own daddy doesn't support her. My father keeps an eye on everything Emily needs. Why can't you do the same?"

Amma always told Urmi that Emily needs a father, so she needed to be nice to him. So when Shahid showed up, even though she was very angry, she accepted him into the house and let him buy another can of milk. After two days he left again. This time Urmi knew not to expect anything from him. And she was not disappointed when she didn't hear from him or get any support for the baby.

She knew she needed to be independent. So she continued looking for a job and started 11th grade again. After six months, Abba's friend helped Urmi get a job as a receptionist at his friend's bank. The office schedule conflicted with her secondary school class schedule. If she remained enrolled in school, she would not be able to work. Abba's friend suggested she get private tutoring and register for the final secondary school test.

Every three months or so, Shahid would show up again and hand Urmi enough money to buy a can of milk or a cheap dress for Emily. Urmi just shook her head. She was married with a child and basically had the responsibility of being a single mother. She couldn't believe her life. When she explained she was working and studying, he would just get jealous because he felt she was becoming successful and he still didn't have a job. Urmi put up with him because she always remembered that Amma said Emily needed a father so people wouldn't talk about her.

The job became unbearable. The men assumed she was single and began hitting on her. Even the old bank manager began following her around. Abba's friend wasn't around because he also worked with the army and had been transferred. Urmi didn't want Abba and Amma to know what was going on because she knew they would worry. After three months Urmi quit but told Abba she was fired.

Urmi was 19 years old and still studying. Now she needed to find another job but she knew it would not be easy. If she could pass the test, she would still be able to get her diploma. Urmi realized this was her only real option because she needed to support her baby.

She started working full time and had a private tutor three times a week for two hours a day.

Amma took care of the baby while Urmi studied and worked. In reality, the job wasn't paying enough to cover the baby's expenses and a private tutor, but it did help the family finances. Amma always encouraged Urmi telling her she would do whatever she needed to do to help her become independent. Amma also realized that Urmi could never depend on Shahid and had to find her own way.

Chapter 5

The Movie Star

One month later was Bangladesh's Independence Day and Urmi sang a song at the neighborhood celebration. A man came up to her after the performance and offered her a modeling job at his agency. She would get paid for every appearance. She wondered if this was Allah's way to provide for her and Emily. It was better than nothing.

Her parents objected. They did not like the idea of their daughter being a model. Abba knew it was against their religion. Urmi didn't think there was anything wrong with the job. She wouldn't be by herself, and she figured she would only be called for one show anyway. It wasn't like a normal 9-to-5 job.

She would do a show and come home with money. She desperately needed money. She felt it would be foolish not to accept the offer. She finally convinced her parents to let her take the job. Her father had only one condition: he had to be with her when she had a show. Urmi agreed this was a good idea.

Her first job was a TV ad and she got three months of her bank salary for one day's work. No way was she going to give up this job. She was so happy. Finally, Emily would have everything she needed. Her suffering was over. Even her parents were convinced that she wasn't doing anything wrong.

Abba still knew that Allah probably wasn't too happy with the job, but Abba understood that Urmi's situation would improve with the high pay. She soon got more modeling jobs. When a TV ad came out, Shahid quickly appeared at her door. He was angry that she had taken this job.

He wanted to speak to Amma, "Why are you letting your daughter make a TV ad? You know this isn't good. She is my wife. She can't take a job like that."

Amma wasn't having it! "What right do you have to say anything about what kind of job Urmi gets? Where's the money to support your baby? When was the last time you cared about whether your baby ate or had the things she needs? When you start taking some responsibility as a father and a husband, then you can say something."

He was very upset and took Urmi and Emily to his parent's house. His parents were so impressed with the ad that she had done. They congratulated her and were so pleased she was able to get some money to support the baby. While they were at his parents' house they lived off the money Urmi made from modeling.

Their money was running out, and Shahid's parents realized he was expecting them to support his family. Shahid's parents explained to him that if his wife and baby were going to live there, he needed to contribute. Shahid still didn't have a job, and they realized this was an unsustainable situation.

They told Urmi not to listen to Shahid. "You need money for your baby. Shahid can't help you, so you need to help yourself. Go back to Dhaka and get more modeling jobs. You will make enough money to raise your daughter. Be wise. Staying here is not wise no matter what Shahid says."

Urmi knew her in-laws were right. She couldn't rely on Shahid, and she needed to look out for herself and Emily. She took Emily back to Dhaka to her parents' house. She let the modeling agency know she was back and looking for more jobs. A few days later there was a knock at the door. Urmi was surprised to see someone from the modeling agency. He was very excited.

"You won't believe what happened. I got a phone call from Shohidul Hoque (a very famous movie director in Bangladesh). He saw the ad, and he wants you for a part in his new movie. You have to come to the agency right away."

Urmi was so excited. She couldn't believe it. She had seen his movies on TV and sometimes in the theaters. She loved them, and now he was asking her to be in one of them. It was like a dream. She was 19 years old and getting the dream job every teenager wants. She immediately called her parents to tell them about the offer.

Her parents were shocked. Their daughter would be an actress. That was worse than being a model.

What a disreputable job! They did not want such a thing for their daughter. They immediately turned down the offer. Urmi was so upset. She told her parents, "I want to do this job. What is wrong with you guys? Everybody wants to be in the movies. That's a dream come true." But her parents would not listen.

A few days later, there was another knock on the door. Urmi opened the door and the stranger introduced himself as Shohidul Hoque. Urmi was shocked and began to shake. She couldn't believe this famous man was at her door. She didn't know what to say. She asked him to come in and take a seat. She offered him some snacks. He said, "I'm here to talk to your parents because I really want you in my movie."

Urmi got her parents and introduced them. Hoque explained that he understood their hesitancy because of the reputation for wild living in the industry. He assured them that he would look out for Urmi, "as though she were my sister. I will make sure everyone respects her." They could come to every shoot so she would never be alone.

He explained that the movie he wanted her for was a family movie and her character would be very nice and decent. He suggested they try one movie and see what they think. Abba was convinced to let her try but was insistent that she only do one movie because she needed to finish her education.

Urmi was ecstatic. She was fine with only doing one movie even though she thought they might agree to another one later. Her dream was coming true. The contract was signed that day. She got the signing money. It was ten months of her bank job's salary. She couldn't believe it. She held the money and was in shock. Finally, her baby would have everything she needed.

When Urmi began working, she was exposed to things she had never seen before. She met the famous movie stars she had always looked up to her whole life. She felt so excited to meet them. But then she saw them getting drunk after work. She had never seen anyone drink before. This was against Abba's religion, and it was never allowed in her house. This was something she had only seen in movies.

The movie stars would behave so badly after they got drunk. Urmi was shocked. An actor even offered to spend the night with her. She couldn't believe it. She went and told the director who said he would handle the situation.

Urmi locked herself in her room for the rest of the night. She sat on her bed crying. She missed her daughter, and she wondered what she was doing in a place like that. At the same time, she felt confused. Yes, in some ways this was a dream come true, but the reality of the life that the stars were living was not what she ever wanted for herself.

She remembered that Abba had always taught her that watching movies was *Haram* and now she was acting in one. How did she end up in this situation? "Allah," she prayed, "what am I here for? Who am I? What do you want me to do? Amma married me when I was 17."

She continued, "You know my desire was to live with my husband and my daughter. My desire wasn't to be rich and famous. I always wanted to finish my education and to live a peaceful, simple life." But Allah seemed not to hear and never answered. She begged Allah to remove her from this movie life. She did not want to continue in this lifestyle anymore.

When the movie was released it became a blockbuster in Bangladesh. Suddenly Urmi became famous. People even recognized her from the movie and greeted her in the streets. Everyone was looking at her and pointing at her. They would stop to talk to her. She couldn't go anywhere without being recognized. She found this very annoying.

Suddenly, she was getting offers from other directors for other movies. She told Amma not to open the door to anyone from the movie industry. She explained that she didn't want to live the life of a famous person.

Shahid came to the house after he saw the movie. He was so angry. He didn't want an actress for a wife. Of course, he still wasn't providing for Emily, so this just annoyed Urmi. He explained that he was going to open a business in Dhaka and he would rent a house where they could live as a family.

This was the first time he had suggested this. She felt Allah had finally listened to her prayers. Shahid rented a small apartment, and Urmi and Emily moved in. Urmi was happy in this new life because she could avoid all the publicity. The media would go to her Amma's house and of course she wasn't there.

One day, Shohidul Hoque knocked on Amma's door because he wanted to speak to Urmi. Amma immediately sent her brother to get Urmi. Urmi respected him enough that she could not ignore him as she had the other directors. He had been very good to her.

She immediately went to her mother's house to see him. Hoque explained that many directors were calling him complaining that Urmi was refusing to do any movies with them. They thought he may have had a contract with her and that was the reason she was refusing. Hoque wanted her to understand the opportunity that was in front of her.

"This is a once-in-a-lifetime opportunity. You will have a bright future; you will have lots of money and be famous. Why are you throwing your future away? You are only 19 years old, and you will regret this later."

"I don't like this lifestyle. I don't want to be rich and famous. I have my husband and my daughter. Peace is better than fame."

Hoque was shocked. "I have never seen anything like this. No one walks away from this kind of opportunity. You are making history." He got up and left when he realized Urmi could not be convinced.

Years later, after she knew Jesus, Urmi realized that Jesus was there with her, giving her the strength to walk away from fame and riches. She felt a peace like she had never felt before as she was making this decision. She realized that even though she had not yet known Him, Jesus had answered her prayers when she was begging Him to help her leave this lifestyle.

Urmi loved her new life with her husband and her daughter, but after three months, Shahid explained to her that he could no longer pay the rent because he couldn't find a business to open. He took her to his parents' house and promised to contribute to the household expenses. His parents agreed to take them in.

This life was very difficult for Urmi. As the daughter-in-law, she was expected to cook and clean. The family was very large, and there was a lot of work to do. It was very hard for Urmi to take care of baby Emily and also study. After two months, she told

Shahid that if she had to continue living like this she would not be able to pass the test.

Amma had already registered Urmi for the test, and she knew she needed to take the time to prepare. Urmi took Emily and returned to Amma and Abba's house. She spent the next six months studying until the day of the test.

The test was three hours long for each subject. Urmi had to test for eight subjects. There was one test a day. Every day she would go into the testing site and sit for three hours. It was incredibly grueling. For three months, she wouldn't know if she had passed. Finally, after three months, at the age of 20, she received her high school diploma. This was the one goal she was not willing to give up. After graduation, Urmi and Emily continued living with her parents, while Shahid lived with his parents.

He continued to show up every three months and give Urmi whatever money he had on him, but he never gave consistent support. Urmi enrolled in college to get her associate degree. She was studying liberal arts. It would take her two years to get the degree. She began working as a receptionist at an export/import company. She was able to buy Emily all the things she needed. She felt such relief that she did not need to ask her parents for anything.

After she graduated, Shahid came for one of his visits. He was very happy and excited , which was very unusual. He pulled out his passport and showed Urmi his visa to go to America and said, "Our problems are over. I will go to America and make some money and support you. But I don't want you to live in your Amma's house anymore, so when I leave for America you have to move to my Amma's house and stay there until I can take you to America."

Urmi was so happy to hear this news. She felt she would finally have a husband who would support her, and her struggles would be over. But she was also sad because she would not see Shahid regularly anymore. It was uncertain when he would be able to return or when he would be able to bring her to America with him.

Urmi and Emily moved to Shahid's parents' house, and Shahid left for America alone. In New York City, he found a steady job and sent money to his parents to help pay for their expenses. For the first time, Urmi felt at peace. After seven years of marriage, this was the way life was supposed to be.

She was being supported by her husband and didn't have to fight for Emily's survival. She was in her in-laws' house, which is where a married woman and her children should live, instead of in her parents' house, which was not the proper place for a married Bengali woman with children to live. When she lived at her parents' house, all the neighbors knew something wasn't right with her husband. This was always very shameful for Urmi.

After three years, Shahid sent for Urmi to come to New York. She began working on the paperwork for the visa. She needed to go for the interview for the visa. She was nervous because she knew they could deny her visa at the interview. One of Urmi's friends told her about an astrologist nearby. The friend explained that the astrologist could tell her what was going to happen at the interview and more about her future. Urmi became very curious about what the astrologist might tell her.

When she found out it was free, she decided to go see the astrologist at his home. He said, "Very soon you will go to a new country, and when you go there you will start a new business. The new business will be very successful. You will have a son, and your husband will fight with you but never divorce you."

He then handed her a piece of paper with some Arabic writing. "Take this piece of paper and keep it wherever you go. Keep it in your purse. Never leave your house without it. Take it with you to the embassy." Urmi was careful to do everything he said.

Leaving little Emily with Shahid's Amma, Urmi came to America alone.

Chapter 6

Life in New York City

"When I arrived at Kennedy airport," said Urmi, "I was so happy to see Shahid again." She ran to him and threw her arms around him, but he didn't respond. He didn't seem happy to see her.

When they arrived at their house, there was no food for her in the apartment. The refrigerator was empty, and he didn't offer to take her out to eat.

"I had just arrived after a 24-hour trip and had only drunk some of the airline's orange juice. I was so scared of the strange foods they served on the plane. I didn't know what was in them. They might even have had pork in them, so I hadn't eaten any of their food.

I was starving!" She finally went to the bathroom and showered, and just cried and cried.

"Isn't there any Bengali restaurant around here in New York City where we can get some food?" she finally asked Shahid. "I'm starving."

Eventually, he took her to eat in a Bengali restaurant. She was too scared of all the strange foods to eat in any other restaurant. Even now, after living in New York City for over 25 years, Shahid still refuses to eat in any other kind of restaurant.

Although Shahid was not loving or tender to her, Urmi was thankful that he had brought her to New York. After 10 years of marriage, this was the first time she lived independently with her husband as a married woman should. Whenever she cooked and cleaned, she tried to show her deep appreciation. She decided to forgive everything that had happened in Bangladesh. She decided this was a new beginning in a new country, and she would start over.

She explained, "I was so grateful, I felt like Allah had taken me out of that famous, rich and nasty lifestyle and had given me something better. Allah had rewarded me for stopping the movie lifestyle and brought me to the USA to a new life with my husband: the life I was craving for all those years in Bangladesh."

She would continually thank Allah for this new life, even though it was between prayer times. This kind of conversation with Allah was very unusual for Muslims, who usually only pray during the prescribed times.

Years later, after she knew Jesus, looking back at this time she realized that Jesus was there with her. He answered her prayers for a normal life with her husband. She realized He was there listening to her grateful prayers that she thought no one could hear.

Urmi tried to pour her love on Shahid that she had felt for the last 10 years. She felt she never had a chance to love him. She would do everything for him. But, as the years passed she began to realize that he saw himself as a king and her as a slave from whom he could demand whatever he wanted.

Urmi returned to Bangladesh for Emily, who was now 8 years old, and brought her to New York. Although Emily spoke no English, she was enrolled in the third grade. Emily learned very quickly and soon caught up with her class.

While waiting together with the other mothers for their children after school, Urmi got to know Mariam, who seemed to be very friendly. The other mothers warned her not to befriend Mariam, because she was a "no-good" person. However, Urmi could not see anything wrong with Mariam, and being that she had no other friends, she became close friends with her.

A year later, Shahid seemed to be distancing himself more and more from Urmi. If she only laid her hand gently on his shoulder in passing, he did not want her to touch him. One day, she saw Shahid shopping alone for new clothes.

This seemed very strange, because Urmi always had to buy everything for him, or they would shop together. He never went shopping alone. Even so, she never doubted his loyalty. She thought he was so deeply in love with her that he would never be unfaithful.

Even though he began spending whole days at a time by himself, Urmi never thought another woman could be involved. Then someone saw him walking on Steinway Street with Mariam.

"Your husband is cheating on you," the person told her.

"I asked him about it," said Urmi, "and he, of course, denied everything." He said he was planning to go to Maryland to a friend's house and spend a night there.

"Oh," Urmi exclaimed. "I'd love to go to Maryland."

"No, no," Shahid said emphatically, "you cannot go. I'm going by myself." But then another person told Urmi that he was going to go with his "best friend."

Urmi prayed every day. "Allah, what is wrong with my husband? I do not want to believe something that isn't true. Please give me some kind of proof, if this is really true."

Urmi was now pregnant with their son, Yeasin. One day Shahid asked if she could go for her doctor's appointment without him. "I'm very busy at work and can't get off today," he said. When she got home, she called him at work to tell him about her doctor's appointment. The manager told her that he had not come to work at all; he had taken the whole day off.

Urmi was so upset. This was her second pregnancy, and again she felt no support from her husband. He acted so strangely. He wouldn't look at her and acted as though he hated her. He was always angry. He would just push her away. He always wanted to get away from her. Little Emily would look at Shahid and say, "Why do you hate Amma so much? I don't understand."

Urmi would ask Allah, "Why have both of my pregnancies been so miserable? Why is Shahid acting the same way as when I was pregnant with Emily?" Allah never answered her.

Shahid continued to be mean to Urmi, and it was into this environment that little Yeasin was born. Urmi continued praying, "Please, Allah, give me some proof my husband is really cheating on me. I want to have actual proof before I confront him."

Then one day while cleaning, she found a cassette tape with a recording of Shahid and Mariam talking intimately together. Urmi began to cry because she was heartbroken, but she pulled out her prayer rug and thanked Allah for giving her proof. She had been asking for proof for almost two years.

Years later, looking back at this time, she realized Jesus was there with her, giving her the proof she asked for. She was so grateful that her prayers had been answered.

She had prayed for proof, and now she had it. She called Shahid's manager and told him to tell Shahid what she had found on the tape. "Tell Shahid not to come home. If he does, I will call the police.'" The manager was very angry. He fired Shahid immediately, telling him to leave and not come back.

Urmi's Amma was visiting them at that time and tried to console her. "It's OK," she said. "Men do such things. That doesn't mean he'll marry her. It's really OK."

"No, it is not OK! I am going to divorce him!" Urmi insisted emphatically.

A year before this, Shahid had saved a lot of money, and he had given it to Urmi to keep for him in a savings account in her name. Now Urmi decided that she would keep all the money for herself because she needed it for the children. If he could do this, then she did not want to take a chance of being without any money.

"He has to leave right now, and I'm going to get a divorce," Urmi insisted.

Shahid stayed with a friend, but without a job it became complicated. He realized he needed his money. He needed to go and get the money from Urmi, but he was smart enough not to go directly to Urmi, and he waited until she was out of the house. He decided to speak to Amma first, because he figured she would be more reasonable.

"Because of your daughter, I am left without a job. Why is she making things so complicated? She's right, I made a mistake, but men do this. She is being unreasonable, and now I need my money. I gave her some money to hold a year ago, and since she made me lose my job, I need to get my money. You need to talk to her." Shahid was very angry.

Amma explained to him that speaking to Urmi about money right now was not going to work. He needed to restore the relationship first. He had a family and couldn't just throw that away. When the relationship was restored, then he could ask for his money. Shahid decided this was a good idea.

Amma told him to come to the house when Urmi was home. He came and made an even bigger show of how very, very sorry he was; asking her to please,

please, please forgive him, and to take him back. He cried, "When people ask Allah for forgiveness, Allah forgives. You are not bigger than Allah." She recognized the logic in what he said. As a Muslim she understood that Allah forgives when a person asks for forgiveness, but it's important to recite the correct Surah when you ask.

Urmi began to feel guilty because she had to admit she was not bigger than Allah. Since Allah forgives, she should give him a second chance. Eventually Urmi gave in and said she would give him another "second chance" which allowed him to come back, but in reality, in her heart, she had not forgiven Shahid. She was angry and bitter. He wasn't really sorry for the affair either; he just wanted his money back. After he moved back home, Urmi and Shahid began fighting constantly.

Shahid asked Urmi for his money, but she refused to give it to him. She was so angry. She was looking for a way to punish him for what he had done, and holding the money made her feel like she had power over him. She figured as long as she refused to give the money back, then he wouldn't leave, because she knew he loved money more than anything.

Shahid began fighting with Amma as well. He blamed her because Urmi wouldn't give the money back. He thought Amma had told Urmi to keep the money so he would have to come back to the house. Amma decided to find a babysitting job so she wouldn't be in the house all day.

Shahid refused to look for a job. He told Urmi he would only look for a job if she gave him the money back. Urmi said, "I don't care. Then we will live off the money you gave me, and it will be used up quickly. Do whatever you want."

Since neither Shahid nor Urmi were working, they were left without any income. They both stayed at home, fighting all the time. Mariam lived down the block, and Urmi was afraid that Shahid would start an affair again. Every time Urmi thought of that woman she would start yelling at him. She could no longer trust him. Every time he left the house she imagined him running into Mariam.

Shahid was thinking that it might help if they moved out of the city. They started visiting different cities around the United States. Urmi didn't like any of the places they visited. Neither Shahid nor Urmi could drive, so they decided to stay in NYC. A few months later, Mariam moved, but the fighting continued. For one year no one worked and home was just one fight after another. It was a miserable life. True forgiveness never happened.

The money was half gone, and Urmi began to worry about what would happen when it ran out. Shahid continued to insist he was not going to work and support everyone like he had before. Urmi decided to look for an empty store where they could create a business. She figured that between the money she had left and the money she had on her credit cards she could afford to start a store. Shahid agreed to this plan.

A few months later they found an empty store front and opened a small corner store. Both Shahid and Urmi started working at the store. Shahid took two 5-hour shifts and then Urmi took one 8-hour shift. Amma stopped working and started babysitting Yeasin and Emily. The fighting continued, but now they didn't see each other as often.

Shahid began to take money from the cash register every day and save it for himself. The business was under Urmi's name. At the end of the month there was often not enough money for all the expenses. Her debt kept increasing. She was angry at Shahid for taking the money, but he didn't care because he figured he was just taking back his own money that she had refused to give him. This situation continued for years.

Amma returned home. She realized that things were not going to be better and there was nothing she could do to help. After Amma left, Urmi's life became more miserable. Little Emily and Yeasin needed attention, but Urmi was busy in the store.

When it was Shahid's turn to care for the children, he began going out and leaving 13-year-old Emily to take care of 2-year-old Yeasin. Urmi was especially upset by this because Yeasin was born with asthma. Often, she would have to rush Yeasin to the hospital when he could not breathe. This would happen at least once a month. Urmi was always afraid that these attacks would happen while Emily was alone with Yeasin.

Whenever Yeasin seemed to be doing better and Urmi would begin to thank Allah for his health, she noticed that on that very evening his asthma would get so bad she would need to take him to the hospital.

It always felt like some sort of curse to her. She could never be happy when he was better, because there would invariably be a disaster that evening. Urmi began fighting and arguing with Shahid, trying to convince him to stay home with the children until she got home. He was angry and refused to listen.

Urmi became angrier and angrier with Shahid. She did not understand what she had done wrong to have Allah punish her with such a miserable life. She was not the one who had cheated. She finally decided to look for a way to punish Shahid because he was making their lives so chaotic.

Chapter 7

An Unwise Plan

At that time, a new unmarried Bengali man started coming to the store. He brought tea for Urmi and they would talk between customers. She started telling him about the problems she was having with Shahid. After a few months of this friendship, Urmi got a nasty plan in her mind. "It was Shahid who did everything wrong, not me," she reasoned. To avenge herself she devised a plan.

She asked the Bengali man if he would agree to act like her boyfriend. She explained she didn't want to do anything *Haram* (sinful), she just wanted to punish Shahid. She had not done anything wrong, and he would only *act* like a boyfriend. At first, they didn't do anything, other than occasionally go to a restaurant together. Urmi did not try to hide this relationship from Shahid because then it wouldn't be punishment.

She began ignoring Shahid at home. She would ask the man to drop her off in front of their apartment. Shahid quickly noticed she was ignoring him and became suspicious. One day, as Urmi had planned, Shahid noticed her getting out of the man's car. Shahid became angry, and waited for the next time the car stopped by. He began beating the man and ripped off his shirt. Urmi felt a little bad because she had put her friend in a situation where he got beaten up. Shahid was so angry he moved out of the house for two years.

However, Urmi's plan soon backfired. The man began falling in love with her and wanted her to get a divorce and marry him. After a time, he really got very insistent about marriage and Urmi had to tell him, "Absolutely, no!"

Right at that time, Urmi's father came to visit and began to suspect what was happening. He talked with the man and told his daughter, "Urmi, you have children. You cannot do this to them. You need to pray," he said. "You need to practice your religion.

You can never go to *Janna* (heaven) doing this." Abba explained, "After you have children, no other marriage will make you happy and work well. Focus on your children, not on your husband. They need a father."

Abba prayed every day for the family. He prayed that the family would be restored. Abba began looking for Shahid to try and get him to come home. He spoke to Urmi every day about her need to restore the marriage. The situation made Abba very sad.

One day Shahid came to see Abba. He had heard on the street that Abba was looking for him and had said he just wanted to talk. Abba counseled Shahid, "Family is very important. The children need their father. Whatever happened, forgive each other and get back together for the sake of the children."

Shahid felt this was good advice. He went home with Abba to speak to Urmi. Since Urmi loved Abba more than anyone, she could not go against him. Abba said it was the right thing to do to get back together. She trusted Abba and decided to let Shahid come home.

Shahid came back again and she forgave him, she said, "about a quarter of the way." She was still very angry at him. Both of them worked very hard in their store, but their constant fighting continued escalating without a break.

After a year, Abba left for home but his influence remained. Urmi began feeling bad about not practicing her religion like she should. She also knew that she was not praying five times a day like all good Muslims should do. Because of this, she knew she would not be able to escape from hell and go to Paradise. However, following all the Muslim rituals and prayers required a lot of time. She also heard and felt a dark presence in the house. Strange noises kept her awake at night.

She asked Shahid to please take more responsibility at the store, allowing her to have more time at home to pray the five required prayers. But following Muslim requirements was not a priority for Shahid. He refused to give her any time off.

"You live in America now," he said. "Here everyone has to work. This is how it is in America. We can go on Hajj when we get old, and all our sins will be forgiven. Then we can go back to Bangladesh and follow the religious requirements. Don't worry about religion. We are here to make money."

This did not convince Urmi, because she knew life was not guaranteed. It is always possible that you could die tomorrow. She was especially worried because she knew the sin of acting in a movie was very bad. Abba had always told her watching movies was *Haram,* so clearly acting in one was much worse. She was worried that she had not done enough to make up for that sin. And now she had to work so much, she couldn't even do the basic requirements of Islam, much less the extra things to make up for her sin of acting in a movie.

As far as Urmi was concerned, being unable to pray as required was closing the door on Islam, her only hope of escaping hell. She decided to pray the one nightly prayer that she could put into her schedule. But she had also heard that if she prayed for something in the same way for six months, Allah would surely hear and answer.

So after the required prayer for six months, she prayed: "Allah, if you want me to worship you, give me the time to pray! Allow my husband to give me the time off so that I can completely practice my religion with all the rituals and prayers. I want to be in the presence of my creator after I die. I don't want to go to hell." After praying the same prayer for six months she again asked Shahid for more free time. He still refused.

Now Urmi was getting angry with Allah. If Allah commanded her to pray, why wasn't he giving her the time she needed? One day, she got so angry at Allah that she shouted, "Allah, you say I should pray, but I can't get time off to pray. Why don't you do something?"

Urmi was feeling desperate. The door to her Muslim faith was shut, and there was no other way to get to heaven and avoid staying in hell forever! Urmi was also confused. She was beginning to think there must be something wrong with this religion. If Allah wanted her to worship Him and He is all powerful, why wouldn't He change the situation so she could worship?

She wondered if her religion was correct. In this world there were so many religions. If the Muslim religion was the right one, then she wanted to practice it. If she didn't practice her religion, Allah would make her stay in hell.

Why wouldn't Allah give her the time to practice her religion? She cried in desperation, "That's it, Allah.

I can't practice this religion. I shut the door on it! Now You have got to show me how to receive forgiveness for my sins, and how to get to heaven after I die, because I can't find any way. I believe there is a Creator who created me, but I don't know Your name. Are you Allah, Buddha, one of the Hindu gods, one of the Christian gods? I don't know. But from now on, You need to show me the right way."

From that time on Urmi stopped praying the Muslim prayers because she felt there was no point in it. She hoped her Creator would show her the way, but she knew there was nothing more she could do.

Years later, looking back at this time, she realized that Jesus was there with her and heard her prayers that night. Her life was about to take a dramatic turn that could only be orchestrated by her Creator answering her prayers.

Chapter 8

Finding Isa al-Masih

The next day someone rang her doorbell. She looked out and saw two strangers standing at the door. Urmi never opened her door to strangers, but that day something seemed to push her to go and open the door.

The strangers smiled at her and the woman said, "Hi. We're David and Ruthie. What religion do you practice?"

"I'm Muslim," Urmi replied.

"Good. We have a book for you. Have you ever read the *Injil* (Gospel)?" Ruthie asked kindly.

Urmi explained she had heard of the *Injil* but she had never read it. Urmi felt this was very strange. Yesterday she had asked her Creator to show her the way and now someone was bringing her the *Injil*. Could this be the Creator's answer? She made sure the strangers couldn't tell how she was feeling.

The only *Injil* they had was in English, but Urmi wasn't comfortable reading English so she asked for one in Bengali. They promised to bring her one in Bengali the next week. She told them to meet her at the store where she spent most of her time. They left her with a copy of "The Jesus Film" and an English New Testament. For some strange reason, this visit made her very happy.

Little could Urmi imagine how this simple invitation would bring such drastic changes to her life. Ruthie began coming to the store one day a week. They would hang out together while Urmi waited on customers.

"She became my best friend," said Urmi. "Before I felt like a robot. I had no friends, and there was no meaning to my life. I just existed from one day to the next. Being with Ruthie felt so different. When I was with her, I felt a peace like I had never experienced before."

However, Urmi and Shahid continued fighting. Shahid continually threatened to leave her. With Urmi's permission, Ruthie often prayed for them in the name of Jesus and asked many others to pray for them as well. Urmi was beginning to see that there was power in the name of Jesus.

Sometimes David accompanied them when they went out to eat as friends. On one such afternoon, Urmi told them about the time she had gone to the astrologist in Bangladesh. She explained that he gave her a paper with Arabic writing, and said she would leave Bangladesh and begin a business in a far-off land. As long as she kept the paper, he said, the business would be very successful, but she would always have problems in her marriage. After all these years, she was still carrying the astrologist's paper around with her. She pulled it out and showed it to David and Ruthie.

"That did not come from God," said David. "God does not want you to have such problems in your marriage. God wants you to have peace in your home.

Prosperity comes from God, not from an astrologist's paper."

After some thought, Urmi agreed to throw the paper away. David prayed and in the name of Jesus, broke the astrologist's curse of continual problems in their marriage and blessed the business in her store. Together they dedicated the store to Jesus.

However, Urmi and Shahid continued fighting. One day Urmi got so mad at him that she wanted to commit suicide. She called Ruthie who said, "Urmi, don't do it. I'm coming right over to your store to see you."

When Ruthie came over, she said, "Urmi, you can't do anything about this. You cannot change Shahid. Only Jesus can do that. You need to give your life to Jesus so He can work in Shahid's life. Jesus will give you real peace."

That day, after five years of friendship with Ruthie, she prayed and gave her life to *Isa al-Masih*.

"After I gave my life to Jesus, I had a new life," she exclaimed. "Everything felt brand new! The trees looked so beautiful. Everything looked beautiful; even the customers who came to our store looked beautiful! I realized that I had finally found my Creator, the true living God. He had answered my prayers."

That very night, she slept unafraid. The dark presence was gone from their house. Ruthie explained, "Jesus is stronger than any evil spirit. You no longer need to be afraid."

Urmi forgave everyone in her life, including her husband and her Amma. Now she felt a new kind of love for Shahid that was given by Jesus. She began being kinder to him, which made him be kinder as well.

Urmi was confused about this decision. She would stand in front of the mirror and talk to herself. "I asked *Isa* to come into my heart, and I told Him I would follow Him from now on and He would be my boss. What does this mean? Am I a Christian or a Muslim? I think I'm still a Muslim because I was born a Muslim, but I follow Isa. How am I supposed to pray? Should I fast for Ramadan? Do I celebrate my holidays? This is so confusing."

A few months later, NLCC was going on their annual camping trip and invited Urmi to come with them. She had attended the year before with her son and enjoyed it, even though she was not yet a follower of *Isa*. On the last day of the trip everyone brought the food they had left over and put it on the table as a buffet.

Someone had brought a very small pot of rice, about enough to feed two or three people. Urmi and Ruthie were at the beginning of the line, and after getting their food, they sat down at a table facing the buffet table. Urmi watched that little pot of rice expecting it to run out. Everyone took two or three tablespoonfuls of rice, but there was always enough for the next person.

A few days later Urmi said, "Ruthie, did you see that pot of rice?"

"What are you talking about?"

"Everyone served themselves from that little pot of rice and it never got empty!"

"Wow, you're right," said Ruthie, "I wasn't watching, but everyone got rice." When they counted, they realized that 33 people had eaten out of that little pot. They were amazed. Jesus had performed a miracle just like the story of the loaves and fishes in the Bible.

Though Ruthie had never really asked Urmi to attend church, after the camping trip Urmi became very curious about what church was like and started asking Ruthie to take her along. She began going every week, but Urmi thought church was distracting.

"Why is there loud music in church? Isn't a religious service supposed to be quiet and contemplative?" Urmi never mentioned these thoughts out loud because she didn't want to seem rude. She loved the preaching. She loved it when David read from the Bible and then the sermon explained what the Bible said. She always felt the presence of the Holy Spirit.

At the end, Urmi was surprised when David called people to the front who needed prayer. Urmi went to the front every Sunday, and she always felt like some kind of power would go into her when David prayed for her. When she closed her eyes she would see Jesus standing there in a white robe. Later she understood this was the power of the Holy Spirit. She loved this experience and never wanted to miss church.

Although she was experiencing a new life, Urmi still had questions. How was it possible that when she was crying out to Allah for a way to practice her religion, she had found Jesus? Mysteriously, right at that time a book came to their house addressed to a previous renter who had lived there 15 years earlier. The book was entitled *10 Amazing Muslims Touched by God.*[3]

Although Urmi is not a reader, the title sounded so interesting and awakened such a curiosity in her that she finished it in two days. This was the first book she had finished reading since living in the United States.

The book was about ten very dedicated Muslims who, while searching for Allah, had found Jesus. Suddenly she realized she was not alone. She was not the only one who had found Jesus while trying to find Allah. Every story amazed her.

It became clear to her that anyone who truly seeks for God will always find Jesus. She was especially amazed at the story of a father who prepared to kill his son for dishonoring his family by becoming a Christian. He tied him on the back of a donkey as

3   Malic, F. (2012) *10 Amazing Muslims Touched by God.* Shippensburg, PA: Ambient Pre

he prepared to slit his throat. The father intended to parade his son through the village with his slit throat, to show how devoted he was. But just then the donkey kicked, jumped over the fence, and ran away. It stopped running right in front of the Canadian embassy. They rescued him and set him free.

Urmi saw the amazing miracle in what God had done to save his life. In the book she also read about being baptized and began asking what that meant. She was soon ready to take that step.

Chapter 9

The Christianity Box

At first Urmi did not identify herself as a Christian. Instead she saw herself as a Muslim who follows *Isa*. She explained that for Muslims Christianity means men and women living together without marriage, girls not covering themselves, wearing very revealing clothes, kissing in the streets, and basically living a very immoral life such as seen in the basest of movies. She could never see herself as fitting into this "Christianity box."

When she accepted Jesus, it was a very personal decision to give her life to Him. She understood that this prayer was not about a religion; there was no "religion box." She understood that she needed Jesus to transform her life, and she never put her prayer of commitment into a "religion" box.

She understood that by culture she was Muslim, and as a Muslim she followed Jesus, yet she would still fast for Ramadan as was their custom. But as time passed, she realized that she was also free not to follow those customs. Jesus had bought her freedom from all the former obligations of her religious customs and practices.

"Ruthie didn't introduce me to a new religion," she said. "She introduced me to Jesus and explained that I needed to come to Jesus to transform my marriage. But I was still confused about how God could transform my husband's life if he did not follow Jesus. So, I asked them, and David said, 'Don't worry. It is Jesus who will transform his life.' Because of this, Jesus is very personal for me."

For Muslims, a white snake is a symbol of religion. About two weeks after accepting Jesus, Urmi had a dream. She saw people standing all around her, pointing, looking at her and screaming. She saw a white snake had wound itself around her from head to foot, but it was dead.

Everyone was yelling, "Don't move. If you move the snake will become alive and bite you. Then you will die."

"Everyone was so scared of the snake that no one would try to help me. The snake was so strong that no one could do anything. But when I prayed for help, I saw a bright light and a big sword came down and cut the snake off of me."

In Urmi's dream, the white snake, which symbolized religion, was dead. She had never been free to practice her religion; she had always wanted to, but never had the time to do so. Now she realized that if she could have practiced it, the snake would have bitten her. She realized that the bright light was Jesus, and He had cut the dead snake off of her life.

"The night that I accepted Jesus, I slept so well. The night noises and the dark presence in the house were gone. I could begin to relax because Jesus was someone I could depend on."

She remembered that when reading the Qur'an with her father, they read Surah 3:55, which said, "Allah said, 'O Jesus, I am terminating your life, and raising you to Me, and clearing you of those who disbelieve. And I will make those who follow you superior to those who disbelieve, until the Day of Resurrection. Then to Me is your return; then I will judge between you regarding what you were disputing....'"

Suddenly she realized that those people who do not follow Jesus, including Muslims, are the unbelievers who will burn in hell. That day she was very happy because she understood why Muslims had a problem with reading this verse.

"I was very happy because the Holy Spirit gave me this verse. I was wondering what this was talking about. I began to see that if I followed Jesus, my sins were washed away. It was not my virtuous deeds outweighing my bad ones. Jesus was the one who took care of my sins."

Urmi now understood that many people were only Christians in name. It is the person who follows Christ who is a Christian. "Many of the other Christian people I talked to said they didn't even read the Bible or go to church. They were Christian by name but were not followers of Jesus."

She also learned that the Holy Spirit would talk to her. When she was a very new believer, a man from the Jehovah's Witnesses came to her store and asked, "Who is Jesus?"

"God," she answered.

"No," he said, "Jesus is not God. He was just a good man."

She felt very, very confused and called Ruthie. Ruthie simply said, "Pray, and God will give you the answer."

"I prayed," said Urmi, "and God said, 'When you were praying to Allah so desperately, who did I send to your door?'"

"Ruthie."

"'Yes, I sent Ruthie. Not that man. Who did Ruthie tell you Jesus was?' That," said Urmi, "removed all my doubts about who Jesus is. I understood clearly that Jesus is God."

Chapter 10

Shahid

At first, Urmi was very afraid that Shahid would learn that she was a follower of Jesus. He always got angry when she went out with Ruthie. He would tell her that if she continued her friendship with Ruthie, Ruthie would make her a Christian.

She would answer, "What are you talking about? We are good friends. Sometimes we have a conversation about religion, but she never tries to get me to convert. You don't know what you're saying!"

Now that she had made the decision to follow Jesus, she wanted to make sure he did not find out. She was afraid that he would divorce her and leave her like he had always threatened. He would tell her over and over that once he had enough money he would go back to Bangladesh and get a new, younger, uneducated, submissive wife.

Urmi would hide her Bible under her pillow. She would only read it when he was not around. When Ruthie would pick her up to take her to church, she would tell him they were going to drink coffee. She figured she wasn't lying because there was coffee after the service at church which she would drink with her new friends.

One morning, Shahid found the Bible under her pillow. He immediately began to yell at her, "Why do you have an *Injil* under your pillow? Have you become a Christian? What are you hiding from me?"

Urmi answered, "It's just a book I'm reading. It has nothing to do with religion." Shahid did not say anything and just left the house, calmer because he thought everything was ok.

Urmi immediately felt conflicted. She felt God was not pleased with what she had said. She knew He wanted her to tell the truth. She was afraid that God was angry with her. Here she was following *Isa,* and she had no courage to admit it to her husband. That was not being a true follower of *Isa*. She felt very bad.

After one week, she realized she couldn't keep hiding this from Shahid. The conviction got worse every day until she began asking God to help her to tell him. She simply couldn't live with this burden anymore. So finally, she called Shahid over and told him, "Shahid, I have to tell you the truth about the day you found my Bible. I have decided to follow *Isa*, and I have accepted Him into my life. From now on I will follow Him. From now on I don't follow Mohammed anymore."

Shahid exploded, "Finally, you became a Christian. I told you that would happen if you had a friendship with Ruthie. I'm done with you; I divorce you and we are not husband and wife anymore. I did not marry a Christian. I married a Muslim."

Urmi answered, "Why do you care? Why are you so serious about religion? I asked you to give me time to practice Islam, and you wouldn't. And now you're mad, like you actually care about religion. Seriously, you don't even practice Islam. I don't understand why this is so important to you when religion has never been important to you."

Shahid stopped talking with Urmi for a few days and began sleeping in another room. When he started speaking with her again, he angrily told her, "We will stay together for the children and for the business, but we are no longer husband and wife. My sister explained that in the Muslim religion if anyone converts to another religion they are no longer married to their spouse. It is an automatic divorce. When I retire I will definitely go back to Bangladesh and find a good, young, uneducated Muslim wife from the village who will listen to me and take care of me."

Shahid would repeat this to her every day. This was pretty much the only conversation they had. Of course, Urmi was happy that Shahid was not very religious because then he would have beaten her instead of just yelling.

Urmi told Ruthie everything that had happened, and Ruthie prayed for her. Ruthie explained that her faith wasn't in Shahid, it was in Jesus. She could trust Jesus that Shahid wouldn't leave without Jesus allowing it; and Jesus promised that He would take care of her.

After the prayer, she felt the peace of God taking over her heart. She was ready to face another week of Shahid's angry words.

Shahid not only threatened to leave, he also began cursing Jesus with many ugly words. Urmi would get very sad. She would go to the bathroom and cry out to Jesus, asking for His patience and strength to face her husband. She was surprised at how quickly Jesus answered. She explained, "Quickly, not even one minute. It didn't matter how sad I was, He would fill my heart with His peace, and all the pain would go away."

Life continued like this for years. Shahid would constantly say these things, and he didn't care who was there. He would curse her in front of the children, customers in the store, visitors in the house, and other family members. Sometimes he would even say these things to her brother Kamir on the phone. At one point, Kamir strongly encouraged her to leave him.

Urmi was surprised she didn't start hating him again like she used to. This would have been her normal reaction. She had hated him for years. Sometimes she would ask herself, "Why don't I hate him? He is so mean to me. He curses me all the time, and I don't hate him? Why do I love him, and why am I still kind to him?"

She realized she had truly forgiven Shahid from her heart. This was something she was never able to do before knowing Jesus. Then, she had told Shahid she had forgiven him when he came home, but in her heart she was still angry and bitter. Now, she had truly forgiven him.

She realized that Jesus had delivered her from her hatred and had given her a supernatural love for her husband. Even more surprising, He had also removed the hatred for the lady with whom Shahid had cheated. One day she looked at him and realized that he was a new person and she was falling in love with him again. This surprised her, because he was still mean.

She would pray for her husband every day. She especially prayed for his salvation. But Shahid never wanted to hear anything about Jesus. One day, Urmi felt Jesus wanted her to give back the money that Shahid had put in her savings account years ago. Urmi was praying about the situation, and she remembered that a few years before she had bought some gold that she had kept as savings. She got the gold and some other money and gave it to him to repay him. This didn't really change much because he was still angry, but Urmi knew she had obeyed Jesus and that was enough.

Urmi explained that Jesus made her strong, and she was not afraid because she knew Jesus would take care of her no matter what, but she was very sad about the situation. The next Sunday, when she told Shahid she was going to go to church he threatened, "If you go to church, I will go to a prostitute."

"What are you doing in church anyway?" he mocked. "Partying? Singing?" For Muslims, singing is *haram* (something very evil that is strictly forbidden). There was no singing in a Mosque. Singing was wrong! "Christians are crazy if they think they should sing in church. Seriously, how can people go to heaven while singing? Such an easy religion. I know that's the reason you chose this religion. You just want to be able to sing, wear makeup, and not wear the hijab. Your religion is the easy way."

The most important thing in Shahid's life was to make money and to save it for retirement back in

Bangladesh. He wanted to build an apartment building so he could rent the apartments and live off the rent. (He wasn't necessarily sure that he wanted Urmi to be a part of that retirement plan). His ideal lifestyle was that he would work a 12-hour shift and then Urmi would work the other 12-hour shift, so they wouldn't need to waste money on employees.

Like his parents, he considered money spent on the children to be a waste. His father had explained that when they got older, the children would leave anyway. They would have their own lives and wouldn't care for them. This was always an issue when Urmi wanted to spend money on tutoring or things like that.

Urmi insisted on taking Sundays off so she could go to church. This was always a fight because Shahid saw it primarily as a waste of money. When Urmi would suggest a day off for a holiday, it would be another fight.

She suggested they hire an employee for two days so they could have family time, and it was a fight. When they would hire an employee, he always tried to cut their hours and pay them as little as possible. This, of course, caused problems because the employees would quit, or the ones who stayed would steal because they couldn't support themselves on what Shahid would pay. Urmi would get so angry that sometimes she would stop working for a few weeks at a time and let him figure it out.

Nothing really changed Shahid's point of view, and he became more stressed and overworked. He began having panic attacks. He was never at peace. He couldn't sleep at home. He would have a panic attack whenever he was home. Being inside increased his anxiety. Urmi tried to get him to take it easy and take time out of the store, but he refused.

Finally she suggested that he should go to his niece's house and sleep there. There he slept a little better, but the anxiety continued. Urmi told him that if he gave his life to Jesus, Jesus would help him with his anxiety. At that point, Shahid was so desperate to feel better, he agreed to give his life to Jesus. He prayed with Urmi and immediately started feeling better. That night he went home and slept well. Urmi was rejoicing that he had given his life to Jesus.

Chapter 11

The Stroke

Urmi's joy was short-lived. A few weeks later he began fighting with her again about following Jesus. He said, "I'm not following Jesus. You asked me to pray, so I just did what you told me to do. It wasn't my own decision. I only prayed because you said if I prayed the anxiety was going to go away. I don't want to follow Jesus. I never did. I said the prayer because you said it would help."

Life returned to the way it used to be. He worked 12 hours a day, 7 days a week, and tried to convince Urmi to do the same. He continued fighting with Urmi about following Jesus. He would curse Jesus, which would make Urmi especially sad. She loved Jesus, and it made her sad to hear Him treated like that.

Shahid's blood pressure began to go up. The doctors told him he needed to take medication and to stop his insane working hours. He needed to relax and not get so stressed. Shahid would not listen. He wanted to make more money. Urmi finally insisted on getting an employee. She felt it was important to listen to the doctors, even if Shahid didn't think so. She divided the hours among them, and the three of them each worked 8 hours a day, 7 days a week.

Shahid was angry about this. He considered it a waste of money. He made the employee's life miserable. He picked on him, yelled at him and accused him. Finally the employee quit. Urmi refused to pick up more hours and told him to close the store early. Shahid refused and began working 16 hours a day. He wanted more and more money. The fights continued.

One day, Shahid came to the store to start his shift. He walked in and started cursing Urmi and calling her every name he could think of. She didn't say a word, got up, and left the store. As she walked home, she felt so hopeless. She cried out from deep in her heart to

Jesus, "Jesus, I can't handle this anymore. My patience is gone. Do something. Please fix this situation." Urmi and Shahid stopped talking to each other after this.

A few days later, Urmi was surprised when her phone woke her up in the morning. She always turned her phone off to sleep. She looked at the phone and saw that it was her husband calling. Since they weren't speaking she was surprised. She answered immediately. "Please come to the store," he said. "I'm not feeling good. I'm really feeling bad. There is something really wrong. I don't know what it is."

Urmi got up quickly and started walking to the store (a 10-block walk). She tried calling Shahid as she was walking. No one picked up. She called again and again. No one picked up. She immediately knew something was seriously wrong. She called 911 on the way to the store.

When she got to the store, she found Shahid unconscious on the floor behind the register. She tried to wake him up but nothing worked. She put her hand on his chest and began to pray for him. A minute later the ambulance got there and immediately took him to the hospital.

Shahid had had a massive stroke. The doctors explained that he was lucky that he got to the hospital so quickly because they could give him an injection to stop the strokes. They didn't know how bad the damage was to the brain, but it was massive. They would need to wait to find out. Urmi realized that God had intervened when she didn't turn off her phone and had gotten his phone call. If she had turned off her phone as she usually did, she wouldn't have gone to the store until many hours later.

She went home and then returned a few hours later, but he was still unconscious so all Urmi could do was pray. The next day he woke up and the right side of his body was paralyzed. He could speak, but not clearly. The doctors were surprised that he was still coherent. He was completely paralyzed on one side. He couldn't use his arm or leg. He couldn't sit up, much less stand or walk.

Shahid's face was also paralyzed, and food would pour out of one side of his mouth. Urmi saw how scared he was when he realized he couldn't move the right side of his body. She again asked him to follow Jesus and reminded him how Jesus had helped him with the anxiety attacks. She asked him to make a serious decision this time and not go back. Shahid agreed to pray with Urmi. He knew there was hope for him in Jesus, and he was scared. Shahid prayed with Urmi again and gave his life to Jesus.

Many people stopped by the hospital to pray for Shahid and encourage him. He would need many months of therapy. The doctors did not know how much function he would get back in his hands and legs. After a week, they discharged him to go home. He still could not use his arm and leg. Shahid was completely bedridden. He couldn't even get up to use the bathroom. Urmi had to help him use the bedpan, feed him, and everything else while she was still working and taking care of the business. It was completely overwhelming.

Every night Urmi would lay her hands on Shahid and pray for God's healing. Shahid was being very nice to Urmi for the first time in their marriage. Urmi felt God was giving her extra energy and grace to do everything. David would come to the house to pray for Shahid and encourage him. They would read the Bible together.

Urmi paid a physical therapist to come to the house a few times a week for the first month. Slowly Shahid improved enough to go to the bathroom with help and eat if someone served him the food. After he improved a little, Urmi would need to take him every day to physical therapy appointments. As he began to get better, he began refusing to read the Bible with David. He refused to get baptized.

The more his health improved, the more his attitude returned to what it had been in the past. He started denying that he had ever decided to follow Jesus. He said he only agreed because he thought then Jesus would heal him, but since he couldn't walk or use his hand right, there was no point. "You prayed, David prayed, and I gave my life to Jesus. But I still can't walk or use my hand. So what was the point of giving my life to Him?"

After a few months, he began getting upset because he wasn't making money. He couldn't use his right hand at all, and he could barely walk, but he started insisting on going back to work. At first, Urmi would not let him go, but he kept on insisting. At the end of the first year, Urmi spoke to the therapist about Shahid going back to work, and the therapist agreed if he would only go for a few hours and not do too much. Urmi would take him, and he would sit in the store because that was all he was able to do.

He was happy that he was back in the store. He began fighting with Urmi again. He was angry because she would go to work and wasn't always at home when he needed help. He was mad if she paid an employee so she could be at home, and he was mad when there wasn't any money. Urmi felt as though everything made him mad.

Eighteen months after his stroke, he began working behind the register about five hours a day. He learned how to use his left hand for the register. As he became less and less dependent he walked further and further away from Jesus. He finally denied him completely. He began fighting with Urmi about her faith again.

Urmi turned Shahid over to Jesus and decided the stress of Shahid's issues belonged to Jesus and not to her. He would need to take care of him. Urmi's responsibility would be to love him and let Jesus figure out how to change him. Urmi finally reached a place of peace when she left Shahid in Jesus' care.

Chapter 12

God's Calling

God began to show Urmi what He wanted her to do with her new life in Jesus. One afternoon she came home from work and felt unusually sleepy. She laid down and soon was fast asleep.

Suddenly she saw herself in a street but was not there in her body. It was very dark. She asked herself, "Why is it so dark? There is no light here at all except car lights." She tried to cross the street, but it was too dark to see where she was going.

Then the scene changed to a forest, but there was no way to get out of the forest. She called and called, but no one heard her. She felt desperate to get out of the menacing forest.

She was all alone, forsaken, and terribly lost. There was absolutely no one there for her. She was so very scared, alone, and forsaken; she had no phone and no one to call.

Then a voice said, "Call someone to pray for you." It was then that she noticed that in the palm of her hand was an embedded phone. She dialed a number at random and someone answered in Chinese. Urmi cannot speak Chinese, but somehow they could understand each other.

"Can you pray?" she asked desperately. He said he was busy worshiping. "Ok," she said quickly, desperately, "continue worshiping and also pray for me." Then she woke up.

"God," she asked, "What was that about? Please explain it to me so I can understand."

Jesus answered, "I want you to pray for the lost. I gave you that dream to let you know how terrible people feel when they are lost, without Jesus, so you can pray more effectively for them."

Urmi had also read about the gifts that God gives to people to help them lead others to Jesus. She felt the gift God gave to her was the gift of telling others about Jesus. When anyone came into the store with problems, she offered to pray for them in the Name of Jesus.

Urmi asked an old friend, Mustafa, to stop by her store because she had good news to tell him. It was so important she could not just tell him about it over the phone; she needed to talk with him face to face.

When Mustafa arrived, she told him that she had learned the Good News that *Isa al-Masih* would forgive all her sins. By accepting Him, Mustafa could have all his sins forgiven as well. After Mustafa listened to the news that Jesus paid for his sins on the cross, he became quiet and very thoughtful.

"I have lived in this country for 20 years and have worked with many good Christians. They always prayed before their meals, and before making any big decision. I respected them highly for their sincerity and devotion," he said thoughtfully, "but no one has ever told me that if I would give my life to Jesus, God will forgive all my sins. I need to think about this and get back to you. I have never heard this before."

One of Urmi's customers, Monowara (a Muslim from Montenegro), said she was addicted to gambling and was desperate for help. Urmi remembered that she also had once been addicted to gambling. She had asked Jesus to put hate in her heart for gambling. She began to hate gambling and was immediately freed from this addiction. She knew *Isa* had freed her.

"*Isa* can free you from gambling," she told Monowara. "But you will need to invite Him into your heart and give Him your whole life."

Monowara agreed, and Urmi led her to accept *Isa al-Masih*. This was the first time that she led someone to accept Jesus. Monowara's addiction was broken. She immediately ran to her sister Hasina's house and told her about meeting *Isa*. Monowara took Hasina to meet Urmi. And Urmi led Hasina to *Isa*.

After this, Urmi prayed with anyone who had problems. Many had dreams that they shared with her. As people saw the power of praying in the name of Jesus, many opened their lives to him.

"I need to explain something," she told any interested person who came to their store. "Adam and Eve were in the garden, and God's glory was over them. When they sinned, the glory went away, and they were naked. God killed an animal to cover them so no one could see their nakedness.

"Many thousands of years later, *Isa* was the sacrifice for our sins. He covers our sins and washes them away. When we give our lives to *Isa*, His glory, the Holy Spirit, comes in and when we die, He takes us to heaven."

Kamrul was Shahid's friend for many years. He worked as a manager at a restaurant and event hall. He would often invite Urmi and Shahid over. After Urmi got to know Ruthie, they would go to his restaurant to eat. Kamrul and his family would come over to celebrate birthdays and were always over for family gatherings. He was doing very well at his job and felt like everything in life was going well. He had a wife and two children who were doing well in school. He felt as though he was living the American Dream.

One day, he unexpectedly lost his job. The owners of the restaurant had a falling out and lost a lot of money, and Kamrul was laid off. Urmi had already been sharing her faith with him. So when he ended up with problems, he immediately called her and asked for prayer. He began looking for a job everywhere.

Six months later he still had not found a job. He used up all his savings, and his wife got angry with him. She kept yelling at him for not having a job and not providing for the family. His daughter started college and began making friends who did not share the values of the family. She would come home in the early morning. He would argue with her, and with his wife. His daughter left home. His American Dream had fallen apart. He began to think about suicide. He called Urmi, hoping that she could help.

"Urmi, my money is gone. I can't keep living like this. My family hates me. My life is not worth living. Everyone will be better off without me. I think I should die."

"Kamrul, there is a better way. I keep telling you about *Isa*. *Isa* loves you and you refuse to accept Him. Suicide is *Haram* (sin). God will be upset if you commit suicide. Giving your life to *Isa* is a much better choice."

Kamrul thought this was probably a good idea, better than suicide. Urmi invited David and Ruthie to meet with Kamrul and her the next day. That day Kamrul gave his life to *Isa*. Urmi had told him about the miracles *Isa* does, and he was expecting a job any day.

For six more months Kamrul continued to look for a job, and then he decided that following Jesus was useless. Not even Jesus could find him a job. He called Urmi and told her that clearly *Isa* only loved her but not him. He was done with *Isa*.

He decided to start driving for Uber. This was a job he hated, but it was the only thing he could do. He felt like he had no choice. Three months later he called again, upset. He was in the emergency room with a broken hand and could no longer drive. He was so angry, he figured God was punishing him. He was angry at Urmi for convincing him not to commit suicide and telling him that Jesus could help him. He was so angry he hung up on her.

Urmi felt so bad, she began praying for him, asking God why he was suffering so much and why He hadn't provided a job for him. "Why don't you help him, God?"

God said, "You help him."

"But how, God?"

"Give him $500.00," He said.

The next day Kamrul called, and Urmi quickly said, "Before you talk, I need to tell you what God told me. God told me that I should give you $500.00."

Immediately, Kamrul began to cry. "God told you that? Then he really does care about me? I was calling to ask you for money to help pay a bill that's due today on my apartment. I need to pay it or lose my apartment, and I have no money. God knew that and talked to you about this before I even called you? How did He know what I needed? How did He know I needed exactly $500.00?"

"Yes, and that is why I said that I first had to tell you what God said before you could even say anything. That way you would know that this comes from God."

That day Kamrul recommitted his life to follow Jesus, and he started reading the Bible. Since he didn't have a job and his hand was broken, he had nothing else to do. Within one month, Kamrul finished reading the whole Bible. He would always call Urmi and talk to her about what he was reading. He was so excited to learn about Jesus and he was falling in love with Him. The suicidal, depressive thoughts disappeared, even though he did not have a job. One day he called Urmi excited because he had finished reading the whole Bible.

A few days later, he got an unexpected phone call. The stranger said, "I am the owner of a restaurant in Queens. I found your resume online. I am very impressed. You are exactly the person I need. I want to hire you immediately. When can you start?"

Kamrul explained that his hand was broken, he couldn't drive, and he could not start right away. The owner said, "That's ok. I will bring the employment contract to your house tomorrow. Sign it and then you can start as soon as your hand is better."

The next day he signed the contract. He couldn't believe the salary. It was much better than his last job and it was a two-year contract so he couldn't be fired. This was a much larger restaurant and a banquet hall that was four times bigger than the last place.

He immediately called Urmi. "You won't believe what *Isa* did for me. He not only gave me a job, but the owner sat down in my living room with a two-year contract. I have been in this country for thirty years, and I have never seen an employer visit an employee's house with a job contract.

"The job has a better salary than I have ever had before. *Isa* waited to give me a job until I finished reading the Bible. I wasn't even worried about it anymore. When *Isa* gives you something, it's bigger than you could ever expect. It's organized and planned out. *Isa* knows what I need."

Chapter 13

Winning the Family for Jesus

For one year, Urmi did not tell any family member in Bangladesh about what she had done. For Muslims, being a Christian means living a degraded life of sexual immorality and lewdness; in other words, everything portrayed in the worst movies. She could not possibly tell her family that she had chosen to become a Christian.

Urmi went home to Bangladesh the summer after she accepted *Isa*. No one knew she was now a follower of *Isa,* and she was very careful not to tell anyone. Abba had a mild stroke and had a small blood clot in his brain. He felt a heaviness in his head, and it was difficult for him to sit up.

At night Urmi would go into his room, rub his head, and pray quietly that *Isa* would heal him. Everyone thought she was just giving him a massage. When she returned to New York, she would call every day, and no one was complaining about Abba's head. Urmi asked him how he was doing, and he said he was fine and his head was fine. Urmi realized that *Isa* had healed him. She didn't tell Abba because she was too afraid of his reaction. No one in her family knew what she had done.

The burden to tell her family grew heavier and heavier. She began to feel bad when she spoke with them because she had not shared her faith yet. A year had already passed. She was so afraid that they would never speak to her again and she would lose her family. But she knew God wanted her to share her faith.

One day she read Matthew 10:37-39: "Anyone who loves his father or mother more than me is not worthy of me; anyone who loves his son or daughter more than me is not worthy of me. And anyone who does not take up his cross and follow me is not worthy of me. Whoever finds his life will lose it, and whoever loses his life for my sake will find it."

She immediately felt convicted. She realized that she loved Jesus. She had given her life to Him, and she did not need to be afraid to share her faith with her family.

She first told her brother, Kamir. He seemed like the safest person to tell. He only asked her one question: "Are you at peace? Did that decision give you peace in your heart?" Since she was at peace, he was fine with it. He explained that he loved her because she was his sister, and he wouldn't mix his religion with his relationship. Urmi felt such a relief to hear this.

However as a good practicing Muslim, he did want to know the proper response to give his sister. He was also worried because he didn't want his sister to end up in hell. The Qur'an teaches that anyone who converts becomes an infidel and will go to hell. He was worried about this because he loved his sister. He went to speak to the Imam at the mosque to see how he would direct him.

"My sister lives in New York City and has become a Christian," Kamir explained to the Imam. "How should I deal with this? Is there a way to bring her back to Islam?"

The Imam explained the proper Muslim way to deal with the situation: "When your sister visits the family again, you must lock her in a room and not give her any food until she returns to Islam."

Kamir was shocked. He couldn't believe this was the proper way to deal with the situation. "Imam, this doesn't make any sense. I know my sister, she will die with her faith and go with Jesus, and I will have become a killer. How does this help my sister? I can't believe Islam teaches this."

Kamir walked out of that meeting totally disillusioned with Islam. He stopped praying five times a day, and he stopped the other Muslim practices. Urmi would tell him, "Even though you are not practicing Islam, you still need a way to come to Allah. You need to follow *Isa*."

Finally, she gathered up enough courage to call her Amma and tell her that she was a Follower of Jesus. Amma was so angry that she slammed down the phone. Urmi kept calling back, and little by little her Amma began to listen until eight months later, she also opened her life to Jesus.

Amma told her, "Whatever you do, do not tell Abba. Don't tell him you follow *Isa*, and don't tell him I decided to follow Him, either. He is very sick and old. If you tell him, he will have a heart attack and die." Kamir had said the same thing. Urmi was afraid they were right. She did not want to be responsible for her father's death.

Abba had become more devout in his old age. He had gone on Hajj (the Muslim pilgrimage to Mecca) a few years earlier, but after Urmi had moved to NYC. This was the highlight of his life. On the first day of the Hajj, the pilgrims walk around a Black Stone seven times. Each time they walk around the Black Stone the pilgrims kiss the stone.

Abba explained that when they kiss the stone the pilgrims believe all their past sins are gone. Of course, the crowds are so large that many people are not able to get close enough to kiss the stone. So they are allowed to just point to the stone or wave at it. When it was Abba's turn to kiss the stone he couldn't get close enough, so he waved at the stone, and suddenly he felt as though someone was holding his hands. They felt very heavy. It was something supernatural and holy.

He looked but no one was there. He was thinking maybe it was a blessing. The rest of his life he wondered about that experience. After Urmi began following *Isa*, she wondered if Jesus showed up and grabbed his hands so Abba would not worship the stone.

Though Abba believed his sins were forgiven up until that point, he knew he had not lived a perfect life after returning from Hajj. He was aware that his sins were still accumulating, and he really did not want to go to hell.

He would wake up at 3 a.m. to pray an extra prayer on top of the required five prayers. He would recite the *Surahs* all day long until his mouth was dry. Amma was afraid he would make his health worse. She begged him to sleep all night long and to drink enough water. But He would answer, "My time is too short. I need to prepare for the end. I do not want to go to hell. I must do enough good deeds so my balance scale weighs more on the good side. I wonder if I should do an extra prayer at night."

He would share dreams with Urmi where he was always in a grave. They would frighten him very much. He understood this dream to mean that he would soon die. He was afraid that he hadn't done enough good deeds to avoid hell, even though he had already gone on Hajj. He was still terrified of going to hell.

One day Urmi asked him "What does the Qur'an teach about the forgiveness of sin?" Abba answered, "I only read the Qur'an in Arabic. I do not know what it says. The Imam has taught me that I must do many good deeds and follow the Islamic rituals, and then Allah will decide. I don't know what will happen to me."

Urmi had compassion for Abba. She shared the good news about how she received forgiveness, and now she knows she will go to heaven. Not because of all her good works and how many prayers she prays, but because she has put her trust in *Isa*.

Abba became very angry with her. He told her, "From now on you are dead to me. I have no oldest daughter. I cannot believe my daughter would do this to me. I taught you the right way. Now your way and my way are different. We are on different paths. You are no longer my daughter." That day Abba stopped speaking to Urmi. It made her so sad. If he happened to answer the phone when she called, he would slam it down or give it to Amma without saying anything.

Amma was so angry with Urmi for telling Abba what she had done. He would cry all day. Sometimes he refused to eat. He told Amma, "The daughter I have loved the most. The daughter I begged Allah for. Now she betrayed me. She has left the path I taught her. I cannot believe it." His heart was broken, he cried for weeks on end.

Urmi continued to call her parents. One day, Urmi asked Amma to convince Abba to listen to her; he would not need to say anything, just listen to her. Amma told Abba, "It's your daughter. She wants to talk to you. Just listen to her; you don't need to say anything."

Abba took the phone and listened but refused to talk. Urmi told Abba, "Your blood runs through my veins, and I will be your daughter no matter what.

"Instead of not talking to me, let's make a deal: you pray to Allah that I will come back to Islam, and I will pray to *Isa* that you begin to follow Him. If Allah is stronger, then I will come back to Islam, and if *Isa* is stronger, then you will follow Him.

"So, let's see who wins. Let's read the translation of the Qur'an in Bengali together so we can learn what it says. I will share with you what I learned from the *Injil*. That's better than to keep on being angry." Abba agreed that this was a good solution, because he said prayer is a good thing to do, and he began speaking to Urmi again.

Abba was very sick. He had had another stroke. Urmi was very worried that he would die before he accepted Jesus. She prayed every day that God would have mercy on him and that he would follow Jesus. She often spoke about this to Ruthie, and together they would pray for his salvation.

One day, Urmi told Ruthie about a vivid dream she had about her father. She was standing beside his bed with her family, when he, dressed in shining white clothes, began walking away from her on a glowing path that led to beyond the horizon. Her family was crying, and she told them not to cry because she knew where he was going, and he was going to be ok.

"Oh," said Ruthie, "That means that your father will become a follower of Jesus."

He was also totally blind from glaucoma. He became weaker and weaker. His health deteriorated. The thought of dying continued to terrify him.

To avoid prolonged suffering in hell, he continued to recite the Surahs day and night. Despite his weakened condition, he insisted on praying the required five times a day and the extra prayer at 3 a.m. The sicker he became, the more his terror increased.

One day the doctor told Abba he had a hernia and needed surgery, but he said he was too sick to withstand the procedure. The pain was intense. Kamir asked the doctor what the solution was, and he explained there is nothing he can do and he just needed to go home and wait for death. His pain was so bad that he couldn't stand or walk. Everyone in the family was so upset. When Urmi called they told her everything. She was very sad and asked to speak to Abba.

"Abba, I know the best doctor in the world. He is the best physician. He is the Doctor of all doctors. And you already know Him."

Abba was so surprised, "Who is this doctor? What do you mean I know him? Give the phone number and address to your brother so he can take me there."

Urmi smiled and said, "Abba you know Him, the Qur'an says he healed the blind and deaf. He raised the dead. The doctor's name is *Isa*. In the same way you go to a doctor to receive treatment, you need to give *Isa* permission to come into your life and heal you. He won't heal if you don't ask. Just like a doctor who won't treat you if you don't give permission. *Isa* needs your permission to heal you. You need to invite Him into your heart. *Isa* is not a Doctor who will send you home and say 'Just suffer until you die.'"

Abba thought about this and asked, "How do I give permission to *Isa* to heal me? How can I invite him into my life?" It was the joy of Urmi's life to be able to lead her Abba to *Isa*.

Abba had one request of Urmi: "Do not tell your Amma that I am a follower of *Isa*. She will be very upset." Urmi started to laugh, "Amma said the same thing when she accepted *Isa* into her heart over two years ago." Abba was so surprised and happy to hear this. He was glad he was not alone.

One week later, her brother took Abba back to the hospital. The doctor found his condition so much improved that he would be able to withstand the surgery for the hernia.

Abba wanted to be baptized before the surgery, but his health was still too delicate to leave the hospital. The local pastor helped him into a shower in the hospital, and sprinkling some water on his head, he baptized him in the name of the Father, the Son, and the Holy Spirit.

He came through his hernia surgery very well. Now he identified himself as an *Isa* Muslim (the word Muslim means to be surrendered to God. So, *Isa* Muslim means a man surrendered to God through Jesus). He explains: "Allah is my creator, and Jesus is my Messiah."

Soon after his surgery, Abba told Urmi about an amazing experience he had. Abba, who had been blind for years from glaucoma, woke up at 4 a.m. and saw someone standing beside his bed calling his name. At first, he was very frightened; there was no one in the house who would call him by his first name. But then he thought maybe his vision was being restored because he could see the person standing beside his bed calling him, he could see Amma sleeping beside him; he could see the whole room.

"Ashraful. Ashraful. Ashraful, don't be afraid. I'm *Isa*. From now on, you belong to me. No one can take you away from me. I am going to prepare a place for you when you die. When you leave this world, you will come to me. There will be a big celebration, and I will treat you like a son-in-law."

The message from *Isa* comforted him. Now he knew where he would go when he died and whom he would see.

Urmi told Ruthie about what *Isa* had told Abba. "Wow," said Ruthie. "That comes straight from the Bible. Let me read it to you."

Ruthie read John 14:2-3 "In my Father's house are many rooms...I am going there to prepare a place for you...I will come back and take you to be with me so that you may be where I am."

And John 10: 27-28: "My sheep listen to my voice; I know them, and they follow me. I give them eternal life, and they shall never perish; no one will snatch them out of my hand."

Also John 10:3: "He calls His own sheep by name and leads them out." Ruthie read these verses in English to Urmi. Later that day, Urmi called her father and read the passages to him in Bengali.

"That is exactly what *Isa* told me! Abba exclaimed. "I didn't know it was written in the Bible!"

From that day on, Abba was no longer afraid to die. He was so happy. He removed his Islamic skull cap. This shocked Urmi; she hadn't told him to do that. The Holy Spirit told him to remove the cap. He asked her to teach him how to pray and to teach him about Isa. He was so surprised to learn that prayer was simply speaking to God. He started sleeping through the night. Abba wanted to read the Bible for himself, but he was blind. He was so sad because he couldn't read the Bible.

Urmi asked the local pastor to take him an audio Bible (which only had the New Testament) so he could listen. Abba was so happy. He began to listen to it for six hours daily (two hours in the morning, two hours in the afternoon and two hours at night.). Urmi explained, "He fell in love with the Word." He would share with her everything he had learned. He never grew bored listening to the New Testament over and over.

He said each time he listened, it felt as though he was hearing it for the first time. Now that Abba spent his time listening to the Bible, he was developing an intimate relationship with *Isa*. Urmi would often ask him to pray for her. She would cry when he was praying for her, thinking about how God answered her prayer and the miracle He had done in giving her Abba salvation.

Chapter 14

The Children

As a concerned mother, Urmi wanted her children to give their lives to Jesus. Urmi often prayed with 23-year-old Emily, but until then, she had never accepted Jesus as her Messiah. One day Emily was on a bus with her friend, when a woman, a stranger to them, got on the bus and kept looking intently at Emily.

Eventually the woman came to Emily, looked intently in her eyes, and said, "I can see that you are a good girl. Listen to what your mother is telling you. She is a good woman. It is important that you do what she is saying to you." With that the woman left and

Emily came home. Later she allowed her mother to pray with her to give her life to Jesus.

One week later, Urmi was concentrating in earnest prayer for Emily from 1:00 a.m. to 3:00 a.m. «God," she prayed, "last week Emily made a decision to follow You, but I don't see any changes in her life. Please do something in her life to really change her. I give her to you. I give you permission to do anything in her life that you need to do to change her. Whatever it may be, just do it."

That night Emily, together with her friend, were in a terrible accident. At 3:00 a.m., Urmi received a call from the NYC Trauma Center ICU. "Your daughter was in a terrible car accident. She is unconscious. We are taking her in to examine her now. We don't know what is going on yet. You need to come immediately."

Urmi, sobbing, went out to look for a taxi to take her to the NYC Trauma Center. She was worried because it is very hard to find a taxi at 3 a.m. As soon as she got to the corner of the main street, a taxi stopped to pick her up. She felt it was like a miracle. The driver was an older man with a white beard. He was dressed simply and had a Middle Eastern accent.

When he saw her crying, he asked her with such a tender, compassionate, fatherly voice, "What's going on? Why are you crying?"

"My daughter was in a terrible accident. She is unconscious, and I need to go to the hospital right away." He looked in her eyes with such compassion, held out an orange to her, and said kindly, but with great authority, "Your daughter will be OK. Here, take the orange. She's really OK. Don't worry. Don't cry. She is perfectly OK." Urmi felt such comfort and relief from his words. She felt like Jesus Himself was speaking to her and she immediately stopped crying and her fear went away.

He spoke with such authority that Urmi finally went against her custom of never receiving anything from a strange man and accepted the orange he offered. When she got to the Trauma Center, Emily was being wheeled out of the ICU, perfectly well and smiling.

"Oh, Mom, Jesus was there," she said excitedly. "He gave me new life. I was totally dead. I couldn't breathe. Jesus breathed for me and gave me life." She had been unconscious and didn't know how she got to the Trauma Center. "When I woke up there were twenty doctors looking at me. I didn't know what happened. I felt I was perfectly alright. I couldn't understand where I was and why all those doctors were looking at me. It was very confusing."

After the doctors finished all the tests, they came to speak to Urmi. "When your daughter came to the hospital, she was unconscious. We thought she had internal bleeding and broken bones. Her blood pressure was very low. She was really not doing well at all. We were afraid she would not make it. About half an hour later, she suddenly woke up and was fine. We were surprised that all her tests came back normal. It was like a miracle."

Urmi realized that Emily came back right at the time the old man told her she was going to be OK. Later she realized that he was probably an angel.

Urmi remembered her 1:00 to 3:00 a.m. prayer time. God had taken her prayer seriously and had brought into Emily's life exactly what she needed to become dedicated to Him.

A few days later, Emily was sleeping, and when she started to wake up, she felt someone grabbing her arm tightly to the point that it hurt. The person was whispering in her ear, and it reminded her of when her family would pray surahs over her when she was younger. When she woke up, she went and asked Urmi, "Mom, were you in my room last night? Why did you grab my arm so tight? It hurt."

Urmi answered, "What? Why would I go into your room and grab your arm? That doesn't make any sense."

Emily became very afraid. She knew it was a spirit. Urmi immediately recognized that an evil spirit was trying to take her. She taught Emily to pray, "In the name of Jesus, I plead the blood of Jesus. Cover me with your blood, Jesus. Protect me from the evil spirits."

There was another time that Emily began choking on her food. She couldn't breathe and became very frightened. She called out to Jesus, and immediately, she stopped choking and could breathe again. Urmi later asked her why she hadn't called her. Emily explained that she didn't because Jesus had helped her right away. Emily was baptized almost two months later.

When Urmi had first become a believer, she had read in the Bible that Jesus heals people. She decided to pray every day for Yeasin's healing. His asthma was still a continual problem. He could not play sports, and he loved soccer. This always made him so sad. It broke Urmi's heart to see her son suffer.

He always carried an inhaler with him. His asthma was so bad that to climb the stairs to go to bed, he had to use the inhaler. For almost five months, Urmi laid her hands on him and prayed for his healing daily. Then one day, she noticed that he wasn't using his inhaler to climb the stairs. He said he didn't need it anymore. He no longer carries an inhaler; he is healed from his asthma.

However, when Urmi talked to him about accepting Jesus, he was never ready. He went on a retreat with the church, but he still did not accept Jesus. Yeasin always said that when he was 18 years old, he would read books on the topic and then decide if he wanted to accept Jesus.

"But suppose you die in the meantime?" asked Urmi. "When I die, I will go to heaven. If you die without Jesus, you cannot go to heaven and you would never see me again." With that thought, Yeasin gave his life to Jesus. He wanted to see his mother again. Yeasin and Emily were baptized on the same day. Urmi made sure that Shahid did not find out.

Chapter 15

Urmi the Missionary

Urmi felt a great sense of urgency to share her faith with everyone. She described it like a burning in her heart to share Jesus with others. Every day she prayed, "God send someone to the store today with whom I can share Your good news." When she would walk down the street she would pray, "Lord, use my eyes to see the person with whom You want me to share."

One day Urmi had a doctor's appointment. When the appointment ended and Urmi was about to leave, she suddenly felt that prompting. She needed to share her story with the doctor.

Urmi began the conversation by asking, 'What's your religion?"

"I'm Muslim. I'm from Morocco, and my name is Noorjahan."

"I am an *Isa* Muslim from Bangladesh. I follow *Isa*."

Noorjahan smiled, "I never heard of any Muslim who follows *Isa*. Can you explain that to me?"

"Ok, I will share my story with you."

Urmi shared her testimony with Noorjahan and to Urmi's surprise when she finished her story, Noorjahan began to cry.

Noorjahan said, "You are not here by accident. I found my answer. Now I understand completely."

Urmi was very curious, "What happened? What do you mean?"

Noorjahan explained, "I was born and raised Muslim, but about two years ago I was reading the Qur'an, and I realized that Mohammed was not a good person to follow. I decided in my heart to stop following him that day. I began to meditate at night before I would go to sleep. I would talk to Allah directly and didn't follow the Muslim prayers anymore. I never told anyone about this. Everyone would be very angry if I told them I stopped following Mohammed. I would talk to Allah secretly in my heart.

"About two weeks ago, I was praying at night. Everyone else was asleep. I was in my room without the lights on, and suddenly my room was lit up. I was so scared. I tried to look out the window to see where the light came from. There was nothing there. Then I looked at the ceiling, and I saw Mecca. Over Mecca, I saw a man with a beard. He had a crown of thorns on his head, and his face was covered with blood. Right away I knew this was *Isa*. But this didn't make any sense because Mohammed should be above Mecca, not *Isa*.

"Then the vision ended. For the last two weeks I kept asking myself, 'Why did Allah show *Isa* over Mecca? I don't understand.' Now you have answered my question. You know Mecca is a symbol of Muslims. Now I understand that *Isa* is also for Muslims, not just for Christians."

Urmi asked Noorjahan if she wanted to follow *Isa*. Noorjahan prayed with Urmi and gave her life to *Isa*. Urmi was so happy that God had used her to share the good news.

After Shahid had his stroke, Urmi had to stay in the store until closing time at 3:00 a.m. One night it was so cold and windy that she could not stand outside long enough to wait for a taxi. Urmi saw a pizzeria at the end of their street that was still open, and she quickly went inside to wait.

The owner of the store asked her, "How can I help you?"

"No, no," said Urmi. "I'm just waiting for a taxi to take me home. It's very cold outside."

"Well, while you are waiting can I give you a slice of pizza?"

"No, it's too late for me to eat."

"OK, but it's very cold outside. I'll bring you some coffee," she said.

"No, no," said Urmi. "I need to sleep, and coffee will keep me awake."

"Oh, OK. Then I will bring you some tea. It's on the house."

"OK. I'll have some tea." Urmi answered. In their culture, a person simply could not refuse a sincere offer. It is a blessing to serve others. To refuse something offered would be like stealing their blessing.

To Urmi's surprise, the owner came out with two cups of tea. One for herself and one for Urmi. They sat down and began to share with each other. Urmi felt the prompt of the Holy Spirit. "This is a divine appointment from me."

Halima and her husband, Solayman, were from Turkey. They worked every night in the pizzeria. Urmi felt she should tell Halima her story right then and there, and suddenly all her tiredness was gone. Halima listened and said, "It is not by chance that you are here."

Four years before the night that Urmi took shelter in Halima's pizzeria, Halima read something in the Qur'an that shocked her.

Surah 33, ayat 37: "When you said to him whom God had blessed, and you had favored,

'Keep your wife to yourself, and fear God.' But you hid within yourself what God was to reveal. And you feared the people, but it was God you were supposed to fear. Then, when Zaid ended his relationship with her, we gave her to you in marriage, that there may be no restriction for believers regarding the wives of their adopted sons, when their relationship has ended. The command of God was fulfilled."

The explanation of this ayat was that Muhammad had fallen in love with the wife of his adopted son, Zaid. He decided that it was improper to pursue her, but then Allah revealed this Surah that told him that Zaid was to divorce his wife so Mohammed could marry her. Zaid then proceeded to divorce his wife, and Mohammed married her.

Halima was so shocked that Muhammed would do such a thing that she decided then and there she could not follow him. She was so disgusted by what he had done. She realized that there was no way she would ever find Allah by following this horrible man. This was a complete break from him. It was almost like a divorce.

This left her very confused. She didn't know how to find a path to Allah. She believed that Allah existed but there was no path to find him. She felt lost and did not know what to do. From that day on, when she would go to sleep at night the thought of *Isa* kept coming to her mind, but she didn't know what to do with this. She would ask herself, "Why does *Isa* keep coming to my mind?"

"For four years, *Isa* has been coming to my mind, and now you come, and for the first time I have an answer to my question. I have always asked myself, 'Why do I think of *Isa* all the time?' I finally have my answer." Halima said. "No one has ever told me that about *Isa*. People come by here and give me those little pieces of paper to read, but no one has ever explained what they mean."

Halima was full of questions. A nearby Catholic church had put up a sign about The Most Precious Blood. "What kind of blood is this most precious blood?" she asked.

Urmi explained that Jesus shed his blood on the cross to pay for our sins. That made it "the most precious blood."

"Oh, now I understand," exclaimed Halima.

"Jesus is standing at the door of your heart waiting for you to invite Him in," Urmi explained. "He won't come into your life without an invitation." She thought Halima would invite Him in right away that night. But she didn't.

Urmi closed her store at 3:00 a.m., but Halima and Solayman didn't close until 5:00 a.m. Urmi would go to the pizzeria after the store closed and they would study the Bible together. This gave them a good, quiet time to have a Bible study. By the end of the week, Halima still had not accepted *Isa* as her *Masih* (Messiah). Finally, Urmi asked her, "How long are you going to keep Jesus outside waiting for you to let Him into your life? A good Muslim doesn't leave a person waiting like this."

Halima was quiet for a while and then said, "No, it is not very nice to keep Him waiting so long. I want to invite Him in right now." They prayed together, and Halima accepted *Isa* as her *Masih*.

During one of the CTU prayer meetings, one of the members mentioned he had a neighbor, Emin, who was from Turkey. He had been sharing with him for a few years. He asked everyone to pray because he had cancer. He arranged that Urmi, Halima, and Solayman would visit Emin and his wife, Hatun.

Urmi told him how her Abba had been too sick to have surgery, but after they prayed, he was well enough to have his surgery. Halima shared how she had become a follower of Jesus in Turkish. For the first time, Hatun understood what their English-speaking neighbors had been trying to share with them.

Both Emin and Hatun accepted *Isa al Masih*. Emin began to cry. Urmi was surprised because Muslim men never, ever cry, but Emin sobbed and sobbed and sobbed. On the next visit to his doctor, they could not find one remaining cancerous cell.

Urmi began to ask God to take her out of the store so she could work full time sharing the Good News with others. This was an impossible request. There was no way Shahid could work by himself or find another job if the store was closed. So Urmi kept on praying and waiting for God to answer.

Chapter 16

On to Bangladesh

Urmi wanted to tell everyone about Jesus, not only her friends and people who came to their store, but her whole family in Bangladesh. This included her three brothers, several aunts, a sister living in Germany, an aunt living in England, as well as many nieces and nephews and cousins.

Her brother Kamel worked in Dubai as a taxi driver. Urmi would often talk to him and tell him to follow Jesus. He would always say, "No, I am ok. I don't need to follow Jesus."

One day Urmi answered, "Ok, but since you have to drive for your job, at least let me pray for you, for your protection."

Kamel agreed to let her pray for him. Later that day Kamel was in a very bad accident. He fell asleep while he was driving. He woke up with his car smashed up in a field. He had no idea what happened. He called the police. The police were so shocked that Kamel was not hurt at all. They thought he should have been dead.

The next day he called Urmi and said, "Yesterday I was in a terrible accident. I fell asleep while I was driving. When I woke up I wasn't hurt at all, and the only thing I could remember is that you had prayed for me. Allah saved me. I know that I was saved because you prayed for me. Please pray that nothing worse will happen to me."

"Then you must accept Jesus now so that he can protect you."

"No," was his constant response, even though he knew that Jesus had saved his life. This went on for a few months, and then one time when she called, he did not answer. She called repeatedly, but still got no answer.

Urmi asked Amma if she had heard from him. But she hadn't heard from Kamel either. The whole family was very worried. No one knew what had happened to Kamel. They were afraid that he might have died and no one knew to contact them. Urmi became desperate and cried out to Jesus, "God, please show me what happened to my brother. If he is alive, have him call me. You know everything. I am so worried…"

Suddenly, in the middle of this prayer, her phone began to ring. She looked at the number, and it was from Dubai, but not a number she recognized. She quickly picked it up hoping it was news from Kamel. "Hello, hello, who is this?"

"Hi, my sister, it's me, Kamel."

"Kamel, you won't believe it! I was just praying, begging God to have you call me. This is a miracle. What happened to you?"

"I have only three minutes to talk, so I need to tell you quickly. I am in jail. I didn't have any money to call you."

He had changed to a better-paying job, which was illegal for a foreigner in Dubai. He got a 5-year sentence.

"Now you are in two jails," Urmi told him. "One inside of you and one outside of you. If you follow Jesus, he'll get you out of both jails." This time he agreed to pray with her and gave his life to Jesus. There was only one possibility for Kamel to get out of jail. Dubai would have a yearly lottery on Independence Day to release low-level offenders. Kamel knew it was unlikely that his name would be drawn, but he asked Urmi to pray anyway. Several weeks later, he was shocked when his name was drawn in a lottery to be set free. He knew Jesus had once again saved him. On his return to Bangladesh, he was baptized by the local pastor.

Sometime after Kamel was released from jail, his former cellmate found a piece of paper in a corner with a telephone number. Although he did not recognize the number, he felt a very strong urge to call that unknown number.

When Urmi answered, he explained who he was and that he had been sentenced to 14 years in prison. Urmi told him about Jesus who would release him from his internal jail. He prayed with Urmi to accept Jesus. After that, although she tried to call him several times, she lost contact with him.

Another brother, Kamir, together with his wife (a gynecologist), had prayed and prayed to Allah for a child. Eventually they adopted a little boy, who became very, very sick. Although the doctors could find nothing wrong with him, he could hardly eat or sleep. If he could eat anything, it was only a very thin soup. Urmi asked many people to pray for the boy. One day Kamir called to say that his son had not eaten anything at all for two days. "Would you please pray for him?"

"Yes, of course, I will pray for him," answered Urmi, "but as his father, you too must pray for him. Before you pray, you must accept Jesus into your heart and ask him to forgive your sins, and then you can pray in Jesus' name."

Kamir accepted Jesus and prayed for his son's healing. His son is now completely healed. However, Kamir slowly returned to Islam. His wife, Arpa, listens to Urmi when she talks about Jesus, but so far has made no decision to accept him.

Urmi visited her family in December of that year while her father was still alive. In Bangladesh, where Christmas is not celebrated, she decided to have a birthday party for Jesus. She asked a local baker to bake a cake and decorate it with, "Happy Birthday to *Isa*."

"Who is this *Isa* whose birthday you are celebrating? We have never heard of him," they asked. This was what Urmi was waiting for, and she told everyone in the bakery about *Isa al-Masih* and what he had done for her.

When her parents heard about the cake, they invited their friends and relatives to come and celebrate the birthday party. Sixteen people came to the party.

"Who is this *Isa* whose birthday you are celebrating?" everyone was asking. "Tell us about him. We have never heard about him." Urmi spent the evening telling everyone about the birth of *Isa* and that he was the lamb of God who gave his life to pay for their sins and open the direct way to God.

Not everyone was happy with the changes Urmi brought to her family. One distant cousin, on hearing that she became a Christian, said immediately, "If she's a Christian then she must be killed."

At once the family experienced a time of fear when one of her sisters-in-law went to the local Imam and reported that the family was becoming Christian. "Look," her mother cautioned. "All this 'Jesus talk' around here is getting us into trouble. You must be careful with all this 'Jesus talk.'" However, although the Imam visited them, nothing further developed from his visit. Their "Jesus talk" continues.

On that visit, two aunts, a niece and a cousin prayed with Urmi to accept *Isa al-Masih*. Others listened but were too fearful of spouses and family members to take that step. But Urmi was happy; the seed had been sown.

Chapter 17

Full Time Ministry

Urmi continued to pray that she could go into full-time ministry. She wanted the freedom to use her time to share the gospel and teach her friends who came to Jesus. The time spent in the store felt like wasted time.

Often Urmi would count the money at the store and begin to cry. She would cry out to God, "I don't like counting money any more. I want to serve you. I am so tired of spending my time doing this." Urmi would get frustrated when she would be sharing the gospel with a customer and then four or five other customers would come, and she would have to stop. She would cry out to God again, "God, did you see what happened? I am so frustrated. I can't even finish sharing with my customer without being interrupted. I don't want to work in the store anymore. I want to spend my time and energy sharing the gospel. Please give me a way so I can work full time for you."

CTU had raised enough money to give her a quarter salary. Urmi was pleased that she didn't have to spend as many hours in the store, but she wanted more freedom so she could work full time for Jesus. She was overwhelmed by the responsibility of the store. It took so much time and energy, she could not focus on sharing the Gospel.

CTU began working with Urmi to find a way to raise support. They helped her get a portfolio together that she could present to friends. Urmi got the material together but she did not have any idea with whom to share it. She didn't have that many friends in the Christian community, so she began to pray about this. It was all very confusing. She had no idea how to start raising support.

The next week Urmi received a message from a friend who said that a man named Greg Ford would like to meet her and hear her story. He would stop by the store that very day. A few hours later a man who was clearly not from New York stopped in her store. "I'm looking for Urmi. Is that you?"

"Yes, that's me."

Urmi shared her testimony with him. She suddenly realized that she could share with him that she wanted to work full time. She felt as though God said she could share with him. So she pulled out her portfolio that she had finally gotten together just the week before and shared it with him. After she finished, Greg said, "Thank you for sharing your heart. I will pray about it, and I will look forward to meeting you again."

A week later, Greg introduced her to a lady named Betty. Betty had a friend from Dubai, Rihanna, who was in New York to seek treatment for her son who had cancer. Betty had already shared the gospel with Rihanna, and when she heard Urmi's story from Greg she was very interested that Urmi would meet with Rihanna and share her story. A few days later, Urmi met with Betty and Rihanna, and after Urmi shared with Rihanna, she gave her life to Jesus. Betty had recorded the whole conversation and prayer on her phone.

Betty was so excited she immediately went to her church and with Urmi's permission showed the recording to the pastor. A few days later, Greg came back to New York and asked Urmi to meet him and the pastor from Betty's church. He was very moved by the video he had seen.

Urmi met with Greg, Betty, and her pastor Ron Lewis. She shared her testimony and her desire to work full time in the ministry. She explained how frustrating it was for her to work in the store. Ron Lewis immediately asked her how much money she had already raised and how much more she needed.

Urmi explained that she already had raised some money through CTU but needed the rest. This was only the second time she had ever shared her need to raise support. He said, "OK, we are in. Our church will support you. I need to speak to the head of CTU and to your husband."

After meeting with David and Shahid, Ron Lewis told Urmi that they would support her for the rest of the money she needed. She didn't have to raise any more. They asked her when she wanted to start working full time on ministry.

Urmi was shocked. She knew that God had answered her prayers and had provided a way for her to work on ministry full time. She was so excited. She could spend her time sharing the gospel and following up with people.

That May she needed to go to Bangladesh to see Abba who was very ill. (Kamir had called her and told her if she wanted to see Abba alive she needed to come right away.) She decided that she would hire an employee to work her hours at the store, and she would just keep him when she returned in June. Shahid didn't want the store to be shut because it gave him something to do. She agreed to provide the supervision the store needed, but she would no longer be involved in the day-to-day operation of the store.

Urmi explains, "July 1 was my day of freedom: the day I began working full time for the gospel. This was my joy."

One month later, Urmi received a letter from the store's landlord. The landlord had decided to renovate the store and they would need to vacate the premises by August 31. Urmi was shocked. She says, "He is the living God that can see the future. He knew my landlord would shut down the store, and he gave me full-time ministry work right before the store was closed down."

The day she shut the door for the last time, she felt so much peace. Urmi says, "My burden was gone that day. Jesus says in Matthew 11:28, 'My burden is light.' The business was such a burden to me for 18 years. This is true freedom".

"Since I have been working full time for the Gospel, God has blessed my work. Many Muslims have come to Christ and because of the pandemic people's hearts are open to Jesus. We do Bible studies in the park and online. We have started a ministry where we have Facebook ads to reach Bengalis. This has been my joy".

Chapter 18

Abba's Homegoing

When Kamir called Urmi to let her know that Abba was in the hospital and she needed to come right away, Urmi immediately got a ticket to go see him. Although Abba was not doing well, he was so happy to see his favorite daughter that his health improved immediately. He would eat when Urmi was encouraging him,

Urmi noticed that sometimes he didn't quite understand what was going on around him, but He still listened to the audio Bible. Urmi would pray for him while Abba held her hand and he said, "I feel so much peace when you pray for me. I can't explain the feeling

I get when you pray." The family was so surprised at how much he had improved while she was there.

Urmi had to return to New York, and she feared this was the last time she would see him alive. She went in to say goodbye to him and told him she would come back again. She could tell he didn't really understand that she was leaving for New York. Usually he would cry when she left. But this time he didn't respond. She left with a heavy heart. She was sad because she realized he was suffering; he was so skinny and his mind wasn't always clear. She knew where he was going to go when he died. And she knew Abba also knew.

It was six months earlier that Abba had been admitted to the hospital the previous time. But now he was a different man. He was no longer afraid to die. When he was there that time, he was terrified of the thought of his approaching death.

Now he seemed eager to go. He kept calling, "*Isa*, come and get me. I'm ready to go." Since his surgery, he had lived in the love of *Isa;* now he longed to meet Him face to face. "Come, *Isa*. Come and get me. I'm all ready to go."

The doctors and nurses who had cared for him during his previous hospitalization could not understand what had happened to him. They thought he was confused and did not know what he was saying. But he was waiting for *Isa* to come and take him home. So Urmi prayed as she left, "God, either heal him completely or take him home. This suffering makes me so sad." She knew Abba would no longer suffer when he was in heaven. A few months later, *Isa* came and took Abba home. Urmi remembered the dream where she had seen him dressed in shining white clothing and walking toward a very bright light.

Urmi was sad that Abba had left, but at the same time she knew he had accepted *Isa* as his *Masih* and was glad that he could go to heaven to be with Him. But Nasreen (her sister), who lived in Germany with her husband, sobbed and sobbed all day and all night. Nothing could console her.

"But why do you cry so?" asked Amma. "Your sister isn't crying like that."

"Yes, but she has faith and I don't," sobbed Nasreen. She knew that Urmi was expecting to see Abba again. Nasreen did not yet have that hope. Urmi called her that night, and to Urmi's great joy she accepted *Isa al Misah* because she also wanted to see her father again. Nasreen was afraid that her husband would find out, because he is a devout Muslim and very controlling, so she prayed quietly in her heart so he could not hear.

Urmi did not believe that she would be able to go to Bangladesh for her father's funeral because she had just been there a few months before. But CTU decided it was very important that she go as a witness to her family. They decided to sponsor Urmi as their missionary to Bangladesh and gave her the money for the ticket.

"I also want to go to Bangladesh," Nasreen cried, "but my husband won't let me go."

Urmi talked to Nasreen's husband about letting her go, but he would not give permission. Urmi told his daughter to talk to her father and tell him that her mother really needed to go, or she would get sick. When his daughter talked with her Abba, he said "yes." He could not refuse his daughter's request.

Nasreen called Urmi again. She was very upset. "The ticket will cost $1,200, and he can't pay that much. He doesn't want to let me go."

The next time CTU got together for their weekly prayer meeting, Urmi explained the problems Nasreen was having. She could not afford the ticket. CTU prayed specifically that the ticket would not be more than $800.00. A few days later, Nasreen called Urmi, very excited, "Something is happening to the tickets. The price is coming down. The ticket only costs $790." Urmi explained that CTU had prayed that the ticket price would drop to below $800.00. Nasreen also had permission to go. In the end, Nasreen also received a gift for her ticket.

A few days later, Nasreen again called Urmi crying. "My husband is saying I cannot take any suitcases to Bangladesh with me. He says carry-on luggage is enough because I am only going to a funeral. I have so many things here that I want to take to the family that I'm not using. The airline allows me to take two free suitcases, but my husband won't let me."

Urmi said, "Don't worry, we will pray and ask *Isa* to change your husband's heart. *Isa* can do this." Together Nasreen and Urmi prayed in the name of Jesus, that Jesus would soften his heart. Urmi did not speak to her again until they met in Bangladesh.

Amma decided that Abba should be buried in the village of his birth. In Bangladesh when there is a death, it is the custom that the person is buried right away, but after forty days the family invites everyone to eat together and comfort each other, remembering the person who has died. Often if the family has enough money, they give gifts to the poor in the deceased person's name. As she prayed about this, Urmi felt she should give each family in her father's village a blanket. During the winter, the nights get quite cold, and everyone would appreciate a blanket.

The leaders in CTU (Center to the Unreached) prayed and talked this over and decided to send the money for the blankets with her as an outreach to the Bengali people. Giving the blankets would open many people's hearts to listen to Urmi's story.

Urmi had a layover in Dubai and was in the airport waiting to board the next plane to Bangladesh, when a woman wearing a burka (a black robe covering the person from head to toe with only the eyes showing) sat next to her. It is very unusual for Bengali women to wear a burka. Urmi started a conversation with her.

Khatun worked in Saudi Arabia and was allowed to visit her family in Bangladesh every three years. She was on her way to Bangladesh and had a layover in Dubai. As Khatun told her story, she began to cry. Her husband was an alcoholic who would beat her up. She ran away from home with her two children and eventually married another man. This man had no money, so she left her children with him and went to Saudi Arabia to work as a housekeeper.

The family treated her like a slave. They didn't feed her enough food, they would beat her, and the husband constantly tried to get in her bed, so she ran away and found another job with an older couple. They were a little bit nicer. She could not believe that the "holy country" where Mecca was located, and where Mohammed came from, could be so terrible. All the other Bengalis living in Saudi Arabia had similar experiences. It was terrible, not "holy" at all. This completely shocked her.

Urmi began to comfort her with the words from the Bible. She explained that *Isa* had told anyone who was weary and burdened that they should come to Him, and He would give the person rest in their souls.

She shared her testimony and explained how Jesus had given her rest in spite of her difficult life.

She immediately asked, "And how does all this change come about? How does *Isa* get into your heart?" Urmi told her about the sacrifice of Jesus on the cross and asked if she was ready to take *Isa* as *al Masih* and ask Him to come into her life and forgive her sins.

When she agreed, Urmi led her in a prayer to give her life to *Isa* and then downloaded the Bible on her phone, using the airport's WiFi. She was immediately transformed. She became so happy, she hugged Urmi. Her burden was gone.

They both knew that it was not by accident that they had met for the long layover in Dubai. Although they intended to stay in contact after they landed, it was impossible, being that Khatun lived in a very remote part of Bangladesh with very little phone reception.

Abba had previously called the local pastor and asked about having a Christian funeral, but her brother, Kamir, strongly opposed this. "If you give him a Christian burial, I will leave," he protested. "This will be a scandal and everyone will talk about it. People will start persecuting the family. We can't change his funeral."

"But he asked for this himself. He wanted a Christian funeral," they argued.

"I will not allow you to do this to him! If you insist on it, I really will leave."

"Don't argue," said Amma. "He is not here. This is only his body. It really does not make any difference what we do with his body. He is happy with *Isa*." Eventually they decided to give him a Muslim burial, which would also allow the villagers to take part.

When Urmi landed in the airport she was surprised to see Nasreen with her brother Kamir waiting to pick her up. She hadn't seen her sister in three years. She was so happy she hugged and hugged her. Nasreen was so excited to tell her what had happened.

"You won't believe this. I came with two suitcases. Your prayers were answered. I saw three miracles in a row. First, my husband let me come, and you know how he is. Second, the ticket price was reduced by $400.00 to the exact price you prayed for. Third, for no reason, my husband let me come and bring two suitcases with me. I know that *Isa* is real. Praise God."

After a week, Nasreen had to return home. Over the next year, Urmi saw Nasreen grow in her faith. She used to get depressed and suicidal because of her situation with her husband. She would be angry all the time. Now she was happier and at peace. She found a job and she no longer got so upset by what her husband said and did. She was a completely different person. Her relationship with her children also changed. Urmi is so happy to see this.

When Urmi explained to the family about the blankets, the family became very upset. "Do not give out the blankets, just buy a rug for the mosque. The blankets will cause a lot of fights and chaos in the village. What if people from other villages show up and you don't have enough blankets? This will be a big problem."

Urmi answered, "You don't understand, I prayed after Abba died. I felt Allah showed me to give the blankets in the village. I don't have a choice. I must do this."

When the family saw she was determined, they began discussing how this would be possible. Finally one of Urmi's cousins, who grew up in the village, had an idea.

"Get one blanket for every house. There are 160 houses in the village. We will go door to door and hand out one at a time. This way no one will line up to try and get a blanket. We need to do this quickly before rumors start. You cannot be in the village for a long time. It takes eight hours to get there and eight hours to get back.

"We cannot spend the night in the village with someone from America. If they find out you are from America, they will kidnap you for ransom. Everyone in Bangladesh thinks Americans are rich, and I know the people in this village. Also you cannot say *anything* about Isa. There are many radical Muslims there who will be glad to kill you. I'm really serious about this: not one word about Isa."

Urmi and the local pastor spoke about it. They agreed that they would go and pray for each house to which they gave a blanket. This would be like planting a seed that would later bear fruit.

Urmi gave each family in the village one blanket. The villagers were very happy with their warm, fuzzy, snuggly blankets; especially when the following winter was colder than normal. CTU prayed that the Holy Spirit would anoint the blankets and enter each house and give the families dreams about *Isa*.

One of Abba's younger brothers and his son came to visit her from her father's village. They were farmers all their lives and never went to school, so they had never learned to read. This was the fate that Abba had avoided by running away from home. Two years earlier, when she had visited her family, she had talked to them about what *Isa* had done in her life.

Now they wanted to learn more about *Isa al Masih*. They accepted *Isa* in their hearts that day. Urmi wanted to give them a Bible, but they were illiterate. This was the reality of many of the people in that village. Very few could read. She called the local pastor to see if he had an audio Bible, so she could give her uncle and cousin one the next time she saw them.

The Pastor told her the most amazing story. A few months earlier he had traveled to Malaysia for a conference. A missionary had brought 160 solar-powered audio Bibles in Bengali to the conference. When he met the pastor he immediately gave him the Bibles.

At the end of the conference, the pastor packed up the Bibles and flew to Bangladesh. In customs he was stopped and the officer asked him what he had in his bag. The pastor was very worried. He knew that he would not be allowed to bring these Bibles into Bangladesh. If the officer saw all 160 of them, they would definitely be confiscated.

The Pastor took out one and showed it to him. As he was showing it to him, the officer got called away and another took his place. The new officer immediately recognized what the Pastor had. He looked at him and said, "Take your Bibles and quickly get out of this place. I am Christian. God bless you. Get out of here immediately." As quickly as possible, the pastor left the customs area and brought 160 audio Bibles into Bangladesh.

When Urmi heard this story, the number 160 stood out to her. That was the exact number of houses in her father's village. She immediately suggested they distribute them there. The pastor agreed to go back to the village to distribute the Bibles.

Recently Urmi heard that two men in the village accepted *Isa al Masih*, just from listening to the audio Bibles. The local pastors are very busy doing follow-up, baptizing, and discipling new believers. Please pray for this village in Bangladesh as God continues to work.

Appendix A

New Life Christian Center

As part of the New Life Christian Center's (NLCC) Muslim outreach, David and Ruthie Westmeier were trying to find the quickest way to a place they couldn't seem to find. Each one had a different way to get there and couldn't decide which way would be the best.

"OK," said David, "In this apartment building right here beside us, we're going to ring the doorbell with any Muslim name and talk to them."

They rang the bell and waited. Slowly the door opened and a woman appeared. Ruthie smiled and said, "Hi. I'm Ruthie. This is my brother David. What is your religion?"

"I'm Muslim," she answered.

"Good. We have a book for you. Have you ever read the *Injil* (Gospel)?"

The woman seemed to hesitate, but then received the book.

"Read it," said Ruthie kindly. "I'll come back next week and then we can talk about it."

The woman (Umri) said they had a store where she spent much of her time. Ruthie could meet her there. In the coming months, Ruthie spent one day a week just hanging out in the store with Umri.

They had rung Umri's doorbell at random, but it was a part of the New Life Christian Center's (NLCC) Muslim outreach. David had been frustrated with their lack of any effort to evangelize the unreached people groups in NYC. "We can't just walk around the Muslims without talking to them," he said over and over. "They also need to hear the message of Jesus."

NLCC's mother church, *Iglesia Nueva Vida*, (INV), had a Spanish outreach ministry to the Hispanic people in Queens. Although those who attended INV were very concerned about bringing the Gospel to the lost, they were only reaching those who looked like themselves and with whom they could communicate in their own Spanish language.

People coming from the mosque (half a block from their church) filled the street and even sat on the steps leading up to the church doors. When the church service ended, the Christians walked right around the Muslims without even trying to speak to them.

Seeing this, David decided to try to reach them himself even if no one else would go with him. Taking some tracts about the way of salvation, he crossed the street to a group of Muslim men to distribute them.

However, rather than talking about the way of salvation, the conversation ended in discussing whether the Bible was corrupted. The Muslim men informed him that God couldn't have a son and that Jesus was only a prophet, but Muhammed was the last and greatest prophet. Everyone should read his book, the Qur'an, and follow it.

David's interest in reaching Muslims with the Gospel began during his student days in Nyack

College. He worked in a motel where his boss was Muslim. David gave him a Bible and his boss gave him a Qur'an.

He learned that Islam taught that initially everyone goes to hell upon dying. How long they needed to suffer there before being allowed to go to paradise depended on how often they had prayed; if they had declared that Allah was one god and that Muhammed was his prophet; how many virtuous deeds they had done; if they had fasted during the month of Ramadan; or if they had gone on a pilgrimage to Mecca (hajj), and so on.

Allah would balance every person's good deeds on a balance scale against the person's bad deeds (Qur'an: Surah: 101: 5-11, 21:43); the difference in the balance would determine how much suffering the person would need to endure to balance the scale and be allowed to go to paradise. No one knew how much time he needed to spend in hell until after his death, when Allah would give him the verdict (See Qur'an: 19: 67-71).

At the end of his life, even Muhammad did not know what Allah would decide about his destination.

Although Allah is merciful, he is also called *Al Macker* (the biggest schemer or deceiver). Unless he decided to extend his mercy and grace, even Muhammad could not enter paradise. How a person can have the assurance of receiving his mercy and grace is not found in the Qur'an.

The big, troubling question was: How could the Good News be brought to Muslims without falling into those endless, fruitless discussions? Isaiah 40:3[4] says, "In the wilderness, prepare the way for the Lord; in the desert, make a straight highway for our God." In this case, how could a way be prepared for the Lord among the shifting sands of the desert, and a highway made straight through the tree-clogged wilderness of Islam? No one seemed to have the answer.

After much prayer, a prophetic word was given to David: "You must decide what kind of a church you want," he was told. "If you choose to have an ordinary church, you could grow into a big church. On the other hand, if you decide to emphasize reaching the unreached people like the Muslims, you will remain just a small group."

---

4   Paraphrase

David was born in Popayan, Colombia, SA, to Christian and Missionary Alliance (C&MA) missionaries, Karl and Arline Westmeier. He met his wife, Yeins from Venezuela, in the Nueva Vida church. Now they threw themselves into the work at NLCC.

David's sister, Ruthie, a clinical social worker also born in Colombia, returned from two years of teaching English as a Second Language in Tibet and joined the Muslim outreach.

The people at NLCC did prayer walks, had times of fasting (some repeatedly fasting for 40 days), monthly "Church in the Park"[5] events, and weekly door-to-door outreach programs. At the same time, the little group went through times of severe testing. When the mother church needed bigger facilities and sold the building, NLCC moved to a different location. A few months after the move, that location caught fire and burned down. They were forced to move a second time, but a few months later that building was also sold.

Their third move took them to a church where they were told they would be able to rent for eight years. But

---

5 Instead of meeting in a church, meeting in a central place like a park, made it easier to invite Muslim friends.

then the church split and NLCC was asked to leave. With the fourth move, many of the group decided to return to Spanish-speaking churches, while the core who stayed joined the Queens Christian Alliance Church (QCAC), which had the motto to reach the unreached.

However, the question remained: How can the Good News be brought to Muslims in a way that would avoid the controversial, fruitless bypasses and bring them the Good News of what Jesus had done for them?

For a brief time, Ayasha, a Muslim Background Believer (MBB), had joined them in their outreach efforts. She too asked, "How can I reach my people for Jesus? I have asked this over and over. It seems no one can tell me."

For more than a millennium, until very recently, Muslims have been impenetrable with the Gospel in any major way. All over the world, even where Christians and Muslims live side by side, there have been few evangelistic efforts among them.

When asked about this, the underlying concept of most Christians is "No, they have their religion and we have ours. We live peacefully together." To reach them, the Gospel would truly need to be presented "by a path his feet have not traveled before."[6]

To find the way to God for most Muslims is hard indeed, even when they search for it. Yusef's story is not atypical. He had heard about Jesus and wanted to learn more about him. Since there were several churches in the city where he lived, he went to a church and asked, "Tell me about *Isa al-Masih (Jesus the Messiah)*. I want to understand what he is all about."

"Oh, no," answered the pastor. "We have our religion and you have yours. We don't want any trouble here."

Two other churches gave him similar answers. However, because Yusef really wanted to learn more about the way to heaven, he persisted in his search. Finally, in the third church he was given the address of the one Christian in the city who talked with Muslims and answered these kinds of questions. There Yusef finally received the answer to his search and accepted *Isa al-Masih* as his Savior.

6   Isaiah 41:3.

Even missionaries sent to evangelize people in these countries may not reach out to Muslims. When Mary[7], a missionary to North Africa, at home on furlough, was asked how she reached the Muslims in that country, she answered, "Oh, no. We don't work with them. We work among the established churches to help and encourage them, but they need to reach the Muslims themselves."

As in all religions, many secular Muslims are only Muslims by culture and are not practicing their religion. Yet the burning question for everyone is how they can have their sins forgiven and find the straight way to God. "Show me the straight way to God" is in every Muslim's Morning Prayer.

If the Muslim's search is for the straight way to God, and Christians know that Jesus said, "I am the way and the truth and the life. No one comes to the Father except through me" (John 14:6), then why are Christians not urgently telling everyone about the Good News: neighbors, coworkers, immigrants, refugees, and whomever else they may meet?

---

7   All names have been changed for anonymity

The Pact of Umar[8]

In the 7th and 8th centuries, when the Christian lands in the Near East were being conquered by Muslims, Christians were either killed or subjugated to Islamic rule. When Jerusalem was conquered by Caliph Umar in April, 687 AD, the Christians agreed to sign a pact that, in exchange for their lives, they would in no way give any outward sign of their religion in words, posters, music, or in any other way give testimony to their belief. Neither would they try to convert anyone to Christianity, on pain of death.

---

8 For a short summary of the *Pact of Umar* (sometimes *Pact of Omar*) see Appendix B

This was officially accepted[9] by the Christians at the time of the fall of Jerusalem in 687 AD. This pact, called The Pact of Umar, was signed in Jerusalem and is still enforced in many Muslim lands. Historians debate the authenticity of the pact, but people in Muslim lands live under its stipulations and the spiritual impact is clear.

Over the following millennia, Christians who tried to speak to Muslims about the Gospel and thus violated this pact learned that this was very dangerous. Many churches have been burned, and thousands of Christians have been persecuted and martyred.[10]

It has long been held among Muslims that any Muslim who converts to Christianity should be killed immediately. When it became known that Umri had accepted *Isa al-Masih*, a distant cousin immediately commented, "Then she must be killed." This causes a deep-seated fear in those who come to Jesus. They fear talking to people about their newfound peace, especially to their own family members who could betray them.

---

9 https://www.bu.edu/mzank/Jerusalem/tx/pactofumar.htm
10 See www.opendoors.com

Fear of spies being planted in their churches has even caused pastors in Islamic countries to refuse to explain the way of salvation to outside inquirers.

The Pact of Umar seems to have formed a virtual blindness in Christians even to see Muslims as people to whom they should bring the Good News. Their Muslim friends in their communities, in their places of work, or their neighbors are often not "seen" as being someone to evangelize. They are often bypassed, and their houses or apartments are missed when evangelistic efforts are being carried out.

This is what David and Ruthie and the Center to the Unreached (CTU) experienced when they tried to organize weekly Muslim evangelistic street efforts in Queens. There were very many reasons for not going on outreaches besides the normal "I don't have time."

"I can't go; it is not my calling to go to them."

"I can't go; I don't know what to say to them."

"I can't go; they have an accent. I can't understand them."

"I can't go. I'll talk to people like myself. They also need to hear."

A Buddhist Background Believer named Grace[11] told Ruthie of her exciting experience when she gave her life to Jesus. She told of the difference it made in her life to know that her sins were forgiven and the Holy Spirit was living within her.

About 10 years prior to this, she had returned to her home country and led her whole family to Jesus. Since then her family led several other families to the faith and started a church. They, in turn, had branched out and started other churches. Ruthie was also very excited and asked how they were reaching the Muslims in her country.

"Oh, no," Grace answered, suddenly sober. "We never thought of talking to them. They have their own religion and wouldn't want to hear about Jesus."

Ruthie felt very perplexed. Why did she keep hearing this over and over? How was it that Muslims, who lived in America, who had gone through the American school system and spoke perfect English, who lived and worked next to Christians, had never had anyone even mention the Gospel story to them?

---

11 All names have been changed for anonymity.

Ruthie, who had grown up in Colombia, with three years of clinical counseling in Puerto Rico, and two years teaching in Tibet, had learned that when something strange and uncanny happened consistently over and over, there was usually some hidden spiritual root behind it.

It was during a time when NLCC was fasting and praying and seeking light on how to reach their targeted people groups that Ruthie heard of the Pact of Umar. Having worked with families whose parents or grandparents had made pacts with some spiritual entity in exchange for protection, power, love, or wealth, she had found that if anyone from such families converted, they did not progress in their spiritual growth, or would keep falling away from God unless the pact was recognized and broken in the name of Jesus. The problem with the Pact of Umar sounded strangely familiar.

God[12] says that the sins of the fathers are visited in the children to the third and fourth generation, but He keeps His covenant and mercy to a thousand

---

12 The following are excerpts from Westmeier A.M., (2004), *Healing the Wounded Soul, Vol. IV: Healing Wounded Relationships*. Miami: Xulon Press

generations of those that love Him and keep his commandments (Exodus 20:5-6, Deuteronomy 7:9 [NKJV]).

When speaking of the need to break with all pacts or curses over families or persons, people sometimes feel confused and ask, "Aren't we new creatures in Christ Jesus, and isn't all that forgiven?"

Forgiven, yes! From the moment people repent, they are totally and completely forgiven and are free from the condemnation of all sins. But that does not mean that there is no history that can influence the individual or family. It is this history that must be faced and dealt with. God did not tell us that the sins of the fathers are visited in the children in order to make it so. No! God tells us this because He knows it is true and wants us to know about it, so we can break that inheritance.

The kings of Israel who openly practiced Spiritism, even burning their babies as living sacrifices to idols (2 Chronicles 5-7), were most probably Daniel's family, possibly his grandfather and great-grandfather (Matthew 1:10-11). It was during this time that the Glory of God departed from Israel, allowing the

Babylonians to conquer Jerusalem and carry them into captivity.

Daniel had not taken part in the idolatry and was not held responsible for their sins, yet because he was a member of this family and of this nation, he suffered the same fate as all the others in Jerusalem and lived in slavery for the rest of his life. He was a victim of the consequences of the sins of his grandfather and great-grandfather.

On arriving in Babylon, Daniel proposed in his heart not to sin against God (Daniel 1:8), not even if they'd throw him into the lion's den. Yet in chapter 9, Daniel prays, "We have sinned. We have been disobedient;" and so on throughout the whole chapter.

When Nehemiah, who was born in Babylon, returned to rebuild the walls of Jerusalem, he rented a horse and rode around the walls of the city in order to discover the exact damage that had been done in previous generations. He made an exact list of everything he found.

He prayed, "We confess the sins that we Israelites, including myself and my father's house, have committed against you" (Nehemiah 2:11-16; 1:6

[NIV]). By identifying themselves with the sins of their family and nation, Daniel and Nehemiah could open their generational sins, confess them, and break with them.

When the leaders of the church in Jerusalem made that pact with their Muslim conquerors, they did not choose to conquer, "By the blood of the Lamb and the word of their testimony" (Rev. 12:11). Instead of choosing to proclaim the message of the Gospel, they had chosen to save their own lives.

They accepted that they would never evangelize Muslims, not even talk to them in any way about the fact that Jesus said that he was the only way to God, that he was the only mediator between people and God, and that no one can come to God except through him (1 Tim. 2:5). In other words, they, as Christians, would never try to evangelize a Muslim, and if anyone did try, they gave the Muslims the full right to kill that person.

CTU decided that they, as representatives of the church, would acknowledge the pact, repent, and ask forgiveness that they as part of the church had valued their lives more than to conquer by the blood of the

Lamb and the word of their testimony, even if it meant laying down their lives.

They asked Ayasha, as a representative Muslim, to forgive them for not sharing the Gospel with her people and for valuing their lives more than proclaiming the message of Jesus. They asked forgiveness on behalf of the church for entering into the pact. They asked Jesus to open their eyes to see Muslims as people of God's love, and to give to them and to the Church urgency to bring to the Muslims the Good News of Jesus.

It was interesting that three days after breaking the pact, the Christian and Missionary Alliance (C&MA) called to ask how they could help them in their Muslim outreach.

Five years later in 2016, David, Ruthie and Urmi went together to Jerusalem. There, close to where the Pact had been signed, they confessed and asked forgiveness, as representatives of the Church, that in order to save their lives they had entered into the pact with Calif Umar. They asked Urmi to forgive them for not telling her and her people the Good News of Jesus' love and forgiveness and opening the way to heaven and to God.

It was after the church broke the Pact of Umar that NLCC entered a new phase in bringing the message of Jesus to Muslims.[13]

13 All proceeds from this book will go to NLCC (aka Center to The Unreached). *https://www.ctunreached.com/*

Appendix B

A Resume of Excerpts from The Pact of Omar (Umar)[14]

The Pact of Omar (Umar) is basically a list of prohibitions for Non-Muslims, Dhimmis, including Christians, Jews, Zoroastrians, and Samaritans. There were prohibitions against building new churches or rebuilding destroyed churches or synagogues; their worship places could not be higher than the lowest mosque in town, nor their houses higher than the Muslim's houses.

---

14 Halsall, Paul. "Medieval Sourcebook: Pact of Umar, 7th Century." Medieval Sourcebook: Pact of Umar, Fordham University Sourcebook Project, 1996, https://sourcebooks. fordham.edu/source/pact-umar.asp. Accessed 30 September 2021.

No cross could be displayed on their churches, and if a bell or gong was used as a call to prayer, it had to be "low in volume." They dared not raise their voices in prayer, nor carry Christian books in public. Palm Sunday and Easter parades were forbidden.

Funerals had to be quiet and no non-Muslim could be buried close to a Muslim.

Churches had to be ready to shelter any Muslim who needed it. Any non-Muslim was obligated to host and feed any Muslim passing by for three days. It was forbidden to shelter a spy or to tell lies about Muslims. It was obligatory to show deference to Muslims by rising and giving them their seats.

They were prohibited to teach non-Muslim children the Qur'an; to sell alcoholic beverages to Muslims; to raise a pig next to a Muslim neighbor; to preach to Muslims for conversion; or to prevent anyone from converting to Islam if they wanted to.

No one could adopt a Muslim title of honor; engrave Arabic inscriptions on signet seals; or possess any weapons.

Non-Muslims were prohibited from riding animals in the way of the Muslims or using a saddle. The appearance of a non-Muslim had to be different from the Muslims: their clothes (belts and turbans) and hair style had to be readily identifiable. Christians had to wear blue, the Jews wore yellow, the Zoroastrians wore black, and the Samaritans wore red. In this way it was easy to identify who they were.

Non-Muslims were prohibited from buying a Muslim prisoner, or to "take slaves who have been allotted to Muslims." No non-Muslim could "lead, govern or employ Muslims." If a non-Muslim beat a Muslim, his Dhimmi protection rules would be removed.

The people who would live by the rules of the pact, would become Dhimmis. The ruler would provide security for Dhimmis, including the Christian Believers, who followed the rules of the pact.

CPSIA information can be obtained
at www.ICGtesting.com
Printed in the USA
JSHW010548140723
44545JS00002B/3